MURDER IN CHICAGO

A Northwest Cozy Mystery - Book 10

BY

DIANNE HARMAN

Published by: Dianne Harman
www.dianneharman.com

Interior, cover design and website by
Vivek Rajan

ISBN: 9781798022450

CONTENTS

   Acknowledgments

1   Prologue   1

2   Chapter One   7

3   Chapter Two   11

4   Chapter Three   17

5   Chapter Four   24

6   Chapter Five   31

7   Chapter Six   40

8   Chapter Seven   47

9   Chapter Eight   53

10   Chapter Nine   63

11   Chapter Ten   71

12   Chapter Eleven   76

13   Chapter Twelve   84

14   Chapter Thirteen   94

15   Chapter Fourteen   102

16   Chapter Fifteen   109

17   Chapter Sixteen   118

18   Chapter Seventeen   127

19   Chapter Eighteen   133

20	Chapter Nineteen	141
21	Chapter Twenty	146
22	Epilogue	152
23	Recipes	154
24	About Dianne	160
25	Coming Soon	162

ACKNOWLEDGMENTS

To those of you who are taking the time to read this book, thank you!

To those of you who helped get this book published, thank you!

To my family for your ongoing encouragement, thank you!

And to Tom, for everything. Thank you!

Win FREE Paperbacks every week!

Go to www.dianneharman.com/freepaperback.html and get your FREE copies of Dianne's books and favorite recipes immediately by signing up for her newsletter.

Once you've signed up for her newsletter you're eligible to win three paperbacks. One lucky winner is picked every week. Hurry before the offer ends!

PROLOGUE

"Al was nothing short of a king on this earth," the man said. DeeDee and Jake didn't know who he was, but he certainly sounded sincere. He wiped tears from his eyes on the sleeve of his jacket and looked out at the large crowd of people assembled in the church for the funeral service.

He continued, "Al had a heart of gold, and always wanted to help anyone who was in trouble. I, myself, turned to him for help in many difficult moments."

He continued talking for a while about what a great man Al had been. Then he stepped down from the pulpit, and the priest asked Cassie to come to the front. She took a moment to do so, and was trying not to cry as she stepped up to the pulpit.

Sitting in the front pew along with Cassie's children, Briana and Liam, DeeDee felt like she had a hole in her heart. She leaned close to Jake and shook her head, unable to believe what was happening. "This is surreal, isn't it?" she whispered. "It feels like just yesterday we saw him in the Caymans. Totally fit and well, like he had the rest of his life ahead of him. He had all sorts of plans, too. I just can't believe that now he's gone."

"I know," Jake said. "Moments like this are so cruel. It seems so unfair. He was such a great guy."

1

Standing in front of the pulpit, Cassie looked out at the people in the church and began to speak about her late husband. Her head was held high and her chin was tilted up, so that she looked almost defiant in the face of his death, like she would not let the sorrow of Al's death bring her down to its level.

"Al would not have wanted me to break down," she said in an emotional and strained voice. "He would have wanted me to stand firm and be the strongest I have ever been. Sometimes life brings us tragedy, and I can see him on the other side laughing at the absurdity of it all. Before he died, I didn't know if I believed in an afterlife. But now I can feel him, and I can sense his love, which is still there for me.

"Although we won't be able to carry out all the adventures we had planned together, I will go on alone, and I know he'll be watching me." It was only then that she began to well up with tears that flowed freely down her cheeks. Sobbing and crying, she continued, "We weren't married very long, but I have to tell you, Al changed my life in so many ways. Even though he had a difficult past, he had a bright present, and an even brighter future.

"I only hope that everyone who knew him will take his spirit of adventure, kindness, laughter, and generosity, and try to incorporate those traits into their lives. We can never be like Al, because he was one of a kind. But if we each try, we can all be just a little bit more like him and that way we can make the world a better place."

When she finished speaking Cassie stepped down from the pulpit and walked to the pew where DeeDee, Jake, and her children were sitting. DeeDee squeezed her hand with empathy and said, "You are so strong, Cassie. You're keeping it together so well, and I know Al would be so proud of you."

Cassie gave her a small smile. "I need to talk to you later," she said with an urgent look on her face. DeeDee felt concerned. "Is everything all right?" she asked. Then she felt like a total fool because obviously everything was not even remotely all right given that her husband Al had just died. "Oh, oh, I mean..." she said, feeling awkward.

"It's okay," Cassie said soothingly. "I can't talk right now, but don't worry about me. Everything is okay. More okay than you know."

DeeDee's heart swelled in affection for her friend. She was being so brave. After the church service concluded, the burial was to take place in the church's adjoining cemetery, which was located on Bainbridge Island overlooking Puget Sound.

Cassie, her children, and Jake and DeeDee made their way out to the cemetery with the rest of the mourners. DeeDee noticed two men wearing shiny black suits and dark glasses who looked very sure of themselves, like they owned the whole place.

She pointed them out to Jake. "They've got to be Mafia," she said quietly. "Don't you agree?"

Jake looked them up and down. "I sure would think so, because they certainly fit the profile."

They walked on towards the grave site. "You know, I just remembered something," DeeDee said. "I thought Al said he wanted to be cremated, not buried. Do you remember him saying that?"

"You're right. He'd often said that it was so he wouldn't be buried alive, as I remember."

DeeDee's brow crumpled. "Well, he made that statement in kind of a joking way," she said. "This must be something Cassie wanted to do instead." She shuddered at the thought of Jake dying. "I don't know what I'd do in her situation."

"You'll never be in that situation," Jake said. He flashed a smile at her. "You won't get rid of me that easily."

"Stop it," DeeDee said. "Please remember that this is a funeral for our friend, Al, who just died. Really Jake, your joke is in poor taste."

"Sorry," Jake said. "You're right. I just can't believe that it's actually true. As you said, he was alive and kicking the other day. It's weird to think that he just doesn't... exist anymore."

"Yes," DeeDee said. It made her shiver as she thought of how Al had died. He'd died in a boating accident, having fallen overboard and drowned. His fear of water was well-known and even though he'd recently overcome it, he wasn't as strong a swimmer as he believed he was, and by the time the search and rescue team arrived, it was too late.

Spike and Red, his two dogs, were on the boat with him, and thankfully both of them were fine. Red was clinging to Al when he was found.

An eerie silence settled over the assembled group as Al's casket was lowered into the ground. Cassie threw a single white rose on top of the casket. Many of the other mourners were clutching one another, as if they needed proof that they still existed. And even the strongest looking men had a tear or two trickling down their cheeks.

It was only then that the death of Al really hit home for both DeeDee and Jake. They held hands tightly, as if holding on to each other with an iron grip would prevent them from ever being separated by such a cruel fate.

As soon as the first shovelfuls of dirt were placed upon his casket, DeeDee noticed the suspected Mafia men skulking away. It was as if they'd been monitoring something, but DeeDee had no idea what.

Following the burial, refreshments were to be served at Cassie's home, and everyone returned to their vehicles to drive there. Susie, who was taking care of DeeDee's catering company, Deelish, while she and Jake were in Connecticut, had done the catering and put out a huge spread containing many of Al's special foods - pizza, lasagna, steak, chocolate cake, and Al's favorite food since he'd moved to the Seattle area, salmon cakes. There was something for everyone, just as Al would have wanted.

There were also copious amounts of Brut and Moet champagne. DeeDee noticed Cassie nursing a glass of champagne in the corner, looking into space as she nibbled at the edges of a piece of chocolate cake. Briana and Liam sat quietly next to her.

DeeDee went over and sat next to them. She didn't know quite what to say - it was always difficult to know what the right thing to say was at a time like this. She thought about all kinds of questions that were circling around in her mind, but she disregarded all of them.

Asking Cassie if she was all right seemed ridiculous, because of course she wasn't. She also thought asking how she was holding up seemed trite, so she ended up saying, "I'm here for you, Cassie. If you want to talk, I'd be happy to listen. If you don't, I can just sit by you if you'd like, or I can also go away. It's totally up to you and what you need or want."

Cassie looked up at her gratefully. "I can't wait to talk to you when all these people are gone."

DeeDee looked at her with concern. "Do you want me to ask them to leave? You're under a lot of pressure right now. If you'd like me to suggest to the guests that they should be leaving soon so you can have some private time, I can do that."

"I think that would be a good idea," Cassie said. "This has gone on long enough."

DeeDee enlisted Jake's help and they told the guests that Cassie wanted some space, so she could rest and have some private time. They asked people to leave within the hour. Briana and Liam were the first to leave, hoping people would follow their lead.

Eventually all of the guests had trickled out of Cassie's home, many carrying chocolate cake wrapped in silver foil. Some even took pizza, although the cheese had congealed on it and it was getting cold.

Cassie stood at the door, saying goodbye and thanking everyone for coming. When she closed the door on the final guest, leaving only Jake and DeeDee inside, DeeDee expected her to break down into tears and run into her arms for a hug.

Instead she bit her lip, looking a bit worried. "I'm sorry," she said, "for making you both so concerned about me."

"Don't be silly," Deedee quickly said. "You know we'll do anything we can to help you during this difficult time."

Cassie walked over to the staircase and shouted upstairs. "Everyone's gone!"

DeeDee and Jake looked at each other and couldn't figure out what Cassie was doing. They wondered if she was having some sort of a delayed breakdown.

And then Al appeared at the top of the stairs.

DeeDee gasped.

Al grinned. "Ya' look like ya' seen a ghost, DeeDee. So how was my funeral?"

CHAPTER ONE

"Al!" DeeDee and Jake exclaimed at the same time, both in too much shock to say anything else.

Al jogged down the stairs, clearly fit and in perfectly good health. He clapped them both on the back and flashed a grin at Cassie. "Yo! Cassie done good fer me, huh?"

Cassie looked apologetic and squeezed DeeDee's hand. "Sorry, guys. I wanted to tell you, but there was never a good time."

"Ha-ha! Gotcha!" Al said, tickled by their shocked expressions. "Bet ya'll appreciate me a whole bunch more now, right? Did Cassie make a touchin' speech 'bout me?"

DeeDee was laughing by now. "Actually, she did."

"Cassie, you're an outstanding actress. You've missed your calling," Jake said

"Mind telling us what this is all about?" DeeDee asked.

"Ima hungry," Al said. "Could smell all the food from upstairs and was dyin' to come down. Better be some left fer me."

Cassie grinned. "Dying to come down? Al, that's bad. You can't eat your own funeral food. It would be bad luck."

Al shrugged, looking a little more serious. "Nah. Ain't gonna' miss this fer the world."

They followed him into the dining room where he loaded up his plate. DeeDee, Jake and Cassie passed on eating any more food as they were already full from eating earlier. Cassie looked out one of the front windows with a concerned expression on her face and closed the curtains on all the windows facing the street.

"So… Ima gonna' be straight with ya'," Al said without looking at them, focusing instead on his food. "Had to fake my death to buy some time. I'll give it to ya' straight out. Someone's tryin' to kill me. People been droppin' like flies, and I'm next on the list. I got the tipoff from Benny Amato when I met him in the Caymans, but now it's really heatin' up."

"Who's died?" Jake asked.

"Three victims so far," Al said. "Butch Zamora was first. Supposedly he died of an accidental overdose from his prescription medication. Yeah, right. Next to go was Huey Polanski. Fell outta' window while sleepwalkin'. You see, the Mafia guys are great at makin' them 'accidental deaths' jes' naturally occur.

"That's why I made mine an accident, too. If I'da been bumped off, that's exactly the way my death woulda' been framed. Whoever's trying to put my lights out will probably think someone else got to me first. Or maybe they'll really believe it was an accident. But everybody knows when it comes to the Mafia, accidents jes' ain't what they seem to look like."

DeeDee thought about what Al had said. "What about the third murder?"

"Oh, that was Shirley Morris. Killed jes' a few days ago. It was supposedly suicide, but come on, who rams their own hairdressin' scissors through their heart? Don't make no sense. She was found in that salon she runs with a suicide note next to her sayin' she's such a bad person she jes' couldn't live with herself no more."

"Such a bad person?" Jake asked. "What'd she do?"

Al sat down and began to eat his food. "Well, they called her the Black Widow, 'cuz she had so many dead husbands. Five, I think. Her job in the Mafia was to seduce and lure men to their deaths. She spoke five languages too, ya' know."

"A language for each husband," Cassie said, shaking her head.

"Somethin' like that," Al said with his mouth full of chocolate cake.

"What did the police have to say about all this?" DeeDee asked.

"Jes' the usual. Took everythin' at face value," said Al. "Or at least pretended to. They ain't interested. Them police know a mob hit when they see one, and they jes' let the Mafia run its own version of justice. Sure, they pay lip service to an investigation from time to time, but these three were pretty well staged." He looked up at them. "Sit down, sit down," he said, waving his hand. "You're makin' me nervous, and I don't need nothin' more to feel nervous about."

"Who do you think's trying to kill you?" Jake asked. "Have any idea?"

"Nope," Al said. "I'm gonna' go to Chicago to find out. First, I'm gonna' find out who offed Shirley, and hopefully track down who's lookin' fer me while I'm at it. I know I'll be spotted in the city which'll blow my cover, but at least I'll have bought me some time. Jes' hope it's enough."

DeeDee's head was whirling from everything Al had said. "How are you going to get to Chicago?" She'd noted Cassie's haste to close the curtains. "Do you think people are watching the house?"

"Ain't sure," Al said. "I'm leavin' tonight. Dino from next door will take me and Red somewhere in his cigarette boat. Then I'll get a private plane."

"I'm going to catch up with Al and meet him in Chicago," Cassie said with a worried look.

"Why don't you fly back to Connecticut with us?" DeeDee asked. "We could go to Chicago from there. Jake, I think you have to get back to work, right? But I'll come with you, Cassie."

"Thanks Deedee, but you really don't have to. I don't want to put you out."

DeeDee shook her head. "Don't be ridiculous, Cassie. I want to help you and be with you."

Cassie smiled at her gratefully. "Thanks, DeeDee. That means a lot to me."

CHAPTER TWO

Hope Mitchell was about to meet her best girlfriend, Molly, for afternoon tea, thank you very much. Coffee was for common people. She strutted out of the beauty salon with a bouncy new blowout, freshly manicured crimson nails, and her outfit of choice – a black bodycon dress, which tightly hugged her curvy body in a stretchy material that finished just above the knee. A white leather jacket, white patent high heels, and a black and white Armani bag to match finished off her outfit. And of course, there were the obligatory extra-large oversize shades.

Anyone who knew Hope knew she dressed in monochrome colors and monochrome colors only. It was like her uniform. That way all her wardrobe pieces fit together, and she never had to think about making an outfit match. Occasionally she might wear a splash of color, like the Hermes scarf Hank had bought for her. At least he'd done one thing right, she thought.

She hailed a cab and was soon making a grand attention-getting entrance into the palatial marble reception area of the Langham Hotel.

"Hello, Mrs. Mitchell," the doorman said as she walked by him. She gave him only the slightest of a nod. After all, it wasn't proper to converse with working class people. It might bring down her image, since she wanted to be perceived as aloof and out of reach. And it worked.

She found Molly already waiting for her, tapping her nails on the tablecloth in rhythm with the music from the nearby grand piano. Hope liked to keep people waiting for her. It made people think she was busy, when in reality, she had nothing going on in her life except constant rounds of beauty appointments, taking pictures for an Instagram profile that was going nowhere, and meeting various women for afternoon tea or expensive lunches, and always making snide comments so they'd be assured she was the superior one. The occasional charity event broke up the monotony, and inspired a good image. It also helped throw the scent off Hank and his Mafia activities.

Not that anyone would know, she often thought, and bitterly. He's so boring you'd walk down the street without giving him a second glance.

She liked to walk in public with him, though, because every man turned to look at her. "They all want me, you see, Hank?" she'd say. He'd certainly notice and draw her a little closer. His jealousy gave her wonderful ammunition to manipulate him into buying her whatever she wanted, and not pressing her about doing mundane things such as housework, which were, of course, far beneath her.

Keeping people waiting for her also made her feel important, despite the fact she lived in quite an ordinary suburban home – she'd die if anyone saw it – and was in piles and piles of credit card debt for keeping up appearances. She had a few cards (maxed out) that even Hank didn't know about.

"Hello, Molly," Hope said breezily, taking off her white leather jacket and handing it to the waiter who had hurried after her as she'd strutted into the room in her towering high heels. She insincerely said, "I'm so sorry I'm late!"

Molly's smile was sickly sweet. "It's okay, honey. I know you have a super-packed schedule."

"No, not really," Hope said. "I was just enjoying my time in that exclusive new beauty salon on 7th. I'm afraid I drifted away into heaven during my authentic Thai full-body massage and forgot all about the time."

"Never mind," Molly said with the same fake smile still stretched across her face.

Hope nodded at a hovering waiter. "We'll have the full champagne high tea." Of course she didn't make eye contact, of course.

Before long, their afternoon tea arrived. It came with two champagne glasses, a large bottle of Louis Roederer Cristal, and two large cake stands, one with sweet bites and one with savory bites. Of course, there was the obligatory English tea, too, Langham's own brand. Hope thought British afternoon tea was a mark of someone of her station and status in life.

"How's Hank?" Molly asked.

"Fine, fine, thank you," Hope said. "And George?"

Molly laughed a little. "Just wonderful."

Molly was a golf widow, which made her resent Hank. But she didn't hate her husband. Not like Hope hated hers.

"What do you think about Shirley Morris?" Hope asked. She hadn't had a chance to gossip about it yet, and she couldn't wait to do so. "She thought she was Marilyn Monroe, didn't she?" She smirked. "Probably didn't look so Marilynish with those scissors sticking out of her chest."

"Hope!" Molly said, acting shocked, but then she smirked. "Maybe one of those ex-husbands' families caught up with her. Do you think she really killed them all?"

"Probably," Hope said. "I don't really much care." The truth was, she'd always been jealous of Shirley. Many a time she'd fantasized about doing away with Hank, so that she could live the same kind of lifestyle Shirley did. She had always rubbed shoulders with the most dangerous, good looking, exciting Mafia men. And they all loved her. Even the thought of it made Hope's heart burn with jealousy.

"Well, I definitely don't think it was suicide," Molly said. "Apparently she confessed to feeling guilty in some kind of a suicide note they found next to her body. I don't believe it for a second. That woman didn't have the capacity for guilt."

"I know," Hope said, shaking her head in disapproval like she was a paragon of virtue herself.

"It had to be a hit," Molly said.

Hope nodded. "My thoughts exactly." Sometimes Hope had fantasies of Hank being the victim of a hit. Then she could sell the house, take the cash, go to Los Angeles, and snag a rich and exciting husband. But, unfortunately, Hank was so low on the radar with his boring personality that he attracted no attention whatsoever. Unfortunately, there'd be no tragic Mafia widow tale for her to tell.

If she'd been more involved in the Mafia's business, she might have arranged the hit herself. But sadly, Hank had married 'out' of the Mafia. Hope had a normal upbringing in the suburbs of Chicago, and she had no Mafia connections of her own. Her only involvement with the mob was through Hank. She worried that she might ask the wrong person to take out Hank, and they'd tip him off.

"I still feel sorry for her, in a way," Molly said, then took a delicate nibble of one of the cucumber sandwiches.

"Yes, it would be a terrible way to die," Hope said, but she was secretly thrilled. Shirley's very existence had felt like such an insult to her. Hope believed she was far prettier and far more refined, and thus far more deserving of having Mafia men shower gifts and affection and attention on her. "Still, life goes on. People die every day. Especially when the mob's involved."

"Well, that's true," Molly said. "Don't you… don't you ever worry about Hank?"

The concern in Molly's eyes was infuriating to Hope. Molly's husband George had been born into a Mafia family, but had gone 'out of the business' and trained in accountancy to keep himself safe. Hope pitied her for this. "No, not at all," she said icily. "In fact, I wish he'd take more risks and challenges. I find that attractive in a man."

"You always did like the bad boys, Hope," Molly said with a laugh. "That's why I was so surprised when Hank was the one you chose to marry. He's so straight. I mean, George isn't shaking up the world, but at least he has an edge. He's got a commanding attitude that's allowed him to rise to the top of his firm and become the CFO. On the other hand, Hank is a little…. blah, isn't he? No offense, Hope. I don't mean anything bad by it, it's just an observation."

Hope felt so humiliated and rageful she couldn't respond for a moment. Instead she got out her little pocket mirror and reapplied her Chanel lipstick. Then, once she had a perfect red pout, she smiled a dazzling fake smile at Molly and made a tinkly little laugh. "Hank's brilliance lies under the surface," she said, quite unable to believe she was defending him.

"George may be a flashy CFO, but anyone could do that job. I don't mean to belittle his achievements. It must be nice to have a small, unexciting life that revolves around the golf club. That works well for many people. But I would just die if I was trapped in that bourgeoisie world." She saw an angry glint in Molly's eyes, and it made her feel wonderful.

"Just a personal preference. Anyhow, just because people such as yourself aren't familiar with what Hank does, it doesn't mean he doesn't do anything. On the contrary, in fact his work is top secret." She took a sip of her champagne, feeling victorious. She looked over the edge of her glass at Molly. "That's rather exciting in a way, don't you think? I know I like to complain about him, but that's just me being a little snarky. He's a wonderful, wonderful man."

Molly smiled. "Yes, as you've said so many, many times." Hope knew Molly was alluding to all the times she'd complained bitterly about Hank and the boring, slow life they were living.

But Hope couldn't confide in her any longer. There was a major shift happening in their relationship, and Hope found herself withdrawing into her own world.

She clinked her glass against Molly's. "Cheers to Hank! Oh… and CFO George."

Molly flashed a smile back that was as fake as her own. "Hope, you have a little lipstick on your teeth."

CHAPTER THREE

Sabazio Vinaccia, also known as Surly Sab, washed his face with cold water and patted it dry with a towel. Even doing that made him angry. He had once been such a handsome man, but the adoring smiles of beautiful women had long ago come to an end.

The acid attack had come out of nowhere. Well, not quite out of nowhere. If one was in the Mafia, violence was a given. But acid? He'd always been looking over his shoulder, waiting for a possible attack, but he never expected that one. He'd had visions of himself opening his front door and getting a bullet straight to the brain from a waiting gunman. Often, he'd been unable to sleep thinking about it and had clutched his gun in bed at night like it was his favorite teddy bear from his childhood days.

Sometimes he wished he had been murdered. At least it would have been a quick one shot and then everything would have become black. As it was, he'd had more surgeries than he could count which were financed by his high-level drug deals. But even so, people still turned to stare at him when he walked down the street. He'd been used to heads turning when he was a young man, but for totally different reasons.

Where once he'd swaggered down the streets of Chicago like a peacock with his oiled black hair and tanned skin and sideways grin, feeling like he owned the world, now he burned with shame when people looked at him, which made him furious. It was easier to stay inside these days. The only time he went outside was on his way to and from work.

He didn't want anyone to look at him. He didn't want to look at himself, either, so when he'd moved into his new apartment, he didn't install any mirrors.

Sab had broken the mirror in the mansion where he and his wife Victoria used to live, and threatened her with a broken shard of it. "I can still see well enough to kill you!" he'd yelled in her face, pressing the sharp edge against the delicate skin of her neck. When he looked back on the memory, he could still remember her pretty face contorting into fear, her red lipstick looking like blood. He'd grabbed her long dark hair and thrown her down the stairs with it.

He didn't feel any regrets about it whatsoever. Why should he? While he was having dangerous surgeries to reconstruct his face to some semblance of normal, she was having an affair with one of his cousins who had come over regularly to oversee the building of a luxurious swimming pool in Sab's backyard. It was going to have huge boulders brought in by crane, a waterfall, a lazy stream, and underwater lights that could be changed to Victoria's favorite color, deep purple. He'd designed it himself as a special gift to her.

He'd always been on the hunt for ways to please her, because of a simple, and to Sab, deeply shameful truth. He couldn't have children. In their courting days, he and Victoria had imagined having a huge family, just like the ones they themselves had grown up in.

Sab could still remember it now. They'd traveled outside the city for a weekend at a romantic getaway hotel. One night, they were out walking, enjoying nature, holding hands, and looking up at the starry sky.

Victoria had said, "Sab, darling, I want to have as many children as possible." She'd laughed. "Why don't we be like my grandmother back in Italy. She always said, 'Leave the size of your family to God.' Don't you think that's a wonderful attitude?"

Sab had felt it deep down in his heart. "Yes," he'd said. Sab had visions of lots of little dark headed children padding around and screaming and giggling in the palatial mansion they'd picked out, but not yet bought. "I would love to."

The moment they were married, they began trying. Their lovemaking was romantic and passionate and so deeply intimate he was sure they would be together forever. It felt like a made-in-the-stars type of love.

But month after month, Victoria would cry when she would find out she wasn't pregnant. Each month her crying sessions got longer, until sometimes it took her days to find the energy to carry on with normal life. While Sab was out doing his Mafia work, he worried about her. She was becoming more and more despondent. He rushed home at frequent intervals to make sure she was eating and hadn't done something terrible to herself. That was his worst nightmare.

After a year of trying, they decided to see a doctor about it. That began a long round of tests with no conclusive answers for yet another year. Finally, after drug treatments and all kinds of experimental creams and patches and injections, the doctor told them, "I'm sorry, Mr. and Mrs. Vinaccia. Mr. Vinaccia, you will never be able to have children. Your sperm is defective. You are infertile. The only way for your wife to have a child is with a sperm donor."

They'd traveled home from the appointment in their large Mercedes Benz in total silence, as if they were winded by the shock of the punch in the gut life had just given them.

"We won't use a sperm donor," Victoria eventually said. "Will we?"

"No," Sab said, shaking his head. The shame, the very shame it would be to have a child in his wife's womb that wasn't his. He would feel like an outcast in his own home, knowing they all shared blood that he didn't.

Deep down he knew Victoria would have liked to go the sperm

donor route, but she didn't push it. And he was eternally grateful to her for that. That was why he was always thinking about what would make Victoria happy, all the while with guilt and churning shame just below the surface. He frequently told himself he was a failure as a man. There was something deeply wrong with him he reasoned.

But he watched helplessly from the side lines as Victoria grew and blossomed into other interests. She became a godmother to several children, and volunteered at a children's center every Friday in an underprivileged area of Chicago. She hired a personal trainer at the gym and ran a half-marathon. She bought herself expensive gifts, and went on self-development luxury retreats in the Bahamas.

Everything was fine, as it turned out. Yes, the cavernous house was a little echoey and quiet, but they had plenty of time for just the two of them. Yes, she spent money like it was water over a dam, but he was glad to see a smile on her face. Everything was settled, quiet, and stable.

That is until Sab had a beaker of acid thrown in his face by Shirley Morris' last husband, Leo Alfonsi. The infuriating thing about it was that Leo Alfonsi wasn't even meant to be alive at the time he did it. Shirley was supposed to have murdered him by then.

Leo Alfonsi was far too dangerous for his own good. So dangerous that he was becoming a liability, which is why the higher-ups had ordered for him to be taken out of the game. He didn't seem to care if he lived or died. He lost a ton of money, then made a ton of money, then lost it carelessly, as if life was a game. He didn't take anything seriously, and played fast and loose with life.

Shirley was given the order to kill him at a time when he'd gone to Vegas and lost over a million bucks. But she didn't. Everyone in the inner circle knew it was because she was greedy and that she was waiting until he did his next million-dollar deal. She wasn't just killing for the Mafia's benefit – she had her own skin in the game.

So, she hadn't done it. And Leo Alfonsi decided that his next get-rich scheme would be to turn on his own and extort Sab for every penny he had. Under the pretext of a friendly visit, he threatened Sab with acid, trying to use it as a means to extort five million dollars from Sab. But Sab said no, and Leo threw the acid in Sab's face. Sab shuddered as he recalled the sensation of the acid literally eating away at his skin.

Of course, the higher-ups got someone else to kill Leo the following day, while Sab was still in the hospital having the first of several emergency surgeries. Victoria was at his bedside then, and she was the only hope he was clinging to.

But the very night he came home, things were different.

His cousin was there supervising some construction workers in the back yard who were constructing the swimming pool, but he left quickly, saying, "I don't want to disturb you while you settle in." He wouldn't look Sab directly in the eye.

Victoria looked particularly gorgeous that day, with bright red lipstick and a tight leopard-print dress that showed off all her curves. Sab appreciated that she'd made the effort to look good for him. She continued to make an effort over the next few months, more than she ever had before. She cooked him all his favorite meals, made sure he was taken care of each time he went in for another surgery, and spoke to him in sweet honeyed tones.

"Don't look at me. I am a beast now," he'd say.

"No, no, you are not," she'd reply, stroking his hair. "You're still my king, just like you've always been."

But all the time, she was carrying on with his cousin.

Sab found out because he had a headache. Victoria had become accustomed to 'putting Sab to bed' as if he was a young child. Sometimes after surgeries he didn't feel like making his way all the way down the marble staircase, so she'd bring him his dinner in bed while he watched television. Then they'd have a little chat, and she'd close the door and say, "Night-night, Sab."

But that night, the food, a spicy pasta dish, was particularly heavily seasoned, and he'd drained his first glass of water and needed another. He wasn't feeling too bad, as the effects of his latest surgery were wearing off, so he padded out of the bedroom holding his empty glass, intending to go downstairs to the kitchen to fill it up.

He froze at the top of the stairs, looking down at the most horrific sight he'd ever seen, his wife Victoria and his cousin kissing passionately. Sab roared and hurled the glass down at them. It crashed on the marble floor with a huge smashing sound, and shards of glass flew everywhere.

Victoria let out a piercing scream, and Sab's cousin, cowardly as he was, dashed out the front door, running as fast as his legs would carry him.

"Dante!" Victoria had yelled after him, but he didn't come back. Then she turned to face Sab standing at the top of the stairs. "It's not what it looks like, Sab, darling. Please, understand that I…"

"That you what?!" Sab raged. "That you what?!"

"That, well, you can't blame a woman." She was crying by then. "I mean, look at you, Sab! How can I ever go out in public with you again?" She ran up the stairs toward him. "I'm so sorry, but I just… I just can't get past your face the way it is now. I've been trying, but I can't. I feel more like your mother than your wife and life partner."

All of Sab's shame – about his inability to have children, about his face, about everything he was (he'd always been pushed around by his father and older brothers), came to the surface. He turned to the mirror hanging on the wall and pounded his fists into it, sending it crashing down onto the floor in a flurry of shards.

"Sab, no!" Victoria shouted. "You're scaring me!"

Looking back on it, Sab almost wished he'd killed her that night and then gone after his cousin.

Now, the two of them, Victoria and Dante, were living in Florida and she was pregnant with their second child. They'd wanted out of the mob completely. Sab thought of going to Florida to kill them, but since they were in another state and no longer had ties to the Mafia, he decided against it since he doubted he'd survive an intense investigation by the police.

Sab had also started a new career, rising quickly to become a partner in a private investment brokerage firm. But that didn't stop the immense rage from churning inside him, looking for someone, anyone, to blame for what had happened to him.

CHAPTER FOUR

Al and Red arrived in Chicago on a private plane, landing at a small airstrip just outside the city. Benny Amato, the very man who had told Al there was a hit out on him when they'd met in the Caymans, had a cab waiting for him on the airstrip. Al was thankful for that. The less he could be outside in the open, the better.

He wanted to maintain his cover for as long as possible. In preparation, he'd grown a little more stubble than he usually wore, brought plenty of sunglasses with him, and ordered some new clothes on Amazon Prime that weren't his style at all. Since he'd been in Washington, he'd become a fan of bright colors, but this time he'd gone for all black and gray, dull enough so that he'd blend into the crowd. Hopefully none of the mob would recognize him.

He even watched the cab driver warily as he and Red got in, and drew his shades over his eyes. While he was sure that Benny had nothing to do with the hit out on him, he wondered who the cab was booked through. The Mafia managed to get their members into all sorts of disguises.

He sent a text to Benny: This guy gonna' blow me away, Benny? Who is he? Where's he taking me?

Benny shot back a reply quickly: Don't let them make you paranoid, Al, or you'll lose the war. This guy's fine. Non-mob, just a regular guy. Fourth floor, second apartment on the left. 404.

Fine, Al texted back.

The further they drove into the city, the more nervous Al became. He wondered how he'd become trapped in this web. Well, he knew that very well. He'd seen a shady past catch up with ex-mob members more times than he could count. But the thing that burned him most was the fact that Cassie could now be in danger, too.

He'd tried to dissuade her from coming to Chicago, but she was adamant. And, on reflection, he felt she might be slightly safer that way. Or would she? He wasn't sure. He didn't like the idea of her at home alone, with Mafia members maybe watching the house.

Perhaps if they couldn't get to him, they would… He couldn't bear thinking about it, but, at the same time, being by his side, she was also in danger. He had all sorts of horrible visions of people kicking doors in, machine guns in hand, ready to blast Al and anyone who was with him, away.

An immense sense of guilt had been twisting in his gut for a while. He'd felt a mild version of this symptom from the very beginning of his and Cassie's relationship. The shadow of his past wouldn't let him fully enjoy the present or their shared dreams for a bright future. On their wedding day, that knot of guilt had tightened a little more. And now? It was like someone had tied a rope around his insides, and was squeezing them tighter and tighter by the minute.

That was why he was in Chicago. He was determined to find the potential killer, and the evidence. He wasn't going to do it mob style. No. That time was over. Rather, he was going to hand over all the evidence to the police, and fight for the best police protection he could get. Perhaps he and Cassie would have to move to a remote South American village. But if that's what it took to remain alive, then he'd do it in a heartbeat.

Thinking about all this made the ride go faster, and before he knew it the driver pulled up outside a shiny apartment building that gleamed in the sun. They were in one of Chicago's best districts, and the sidewalks were clean and wide. An extremely slim woman with a tiny dog on a leash and a designer handbag strutted by and walked into the building, giving Al all the information, he needed to know about the neighborhood.

"I'll git my bags," he said to the driver, wanting to get away from him as quickly as possible. He put Red's leash on, stepped out of the cab, and rushed to get his bags out of the trunk.

When he arrived at the front door of the apartment building, the stout doorman warily looked him up and down. "And you are?" he asked, with a sneer on his face.

Al realized he looked slightly dishevelled, but his worry made him short-tempered. "I don't have time for this," he said, looking up and down the street. He didn't know whether to use Benny's name or not, or how it had been booked. Anyone could have connections to the mob, and the less information he gave out, the better. "I have friends upstairs waiting for me."

"Is that so?" the doorman said. "Lift up your glasses. Let me look at you."

"What?" Al said.

"You heard me, pal."

"You don't know me. Don't call me pal."

"Sir, don't get aggressive," the doorman said, despite the fact he'd been much ruder than Al had been. He backed up with an arm out, like Al was going to attack him. "Or I'll have to call the police."

Al called Benny. It took a lot of effort not to curse. "Yer' doorman don't think I'm fancy enough for this buildin'."

"Oh, yeah, he's an absolute clown," Benny said. "Wait there."

With Red attached to his leash, Al strolled away from the building over to the edge of the street, and then walked back again, feeling nervous. A couple of minutes later, he leaned against the wall next to the entrance, his shades still resolutely down.

"I'm going to have to ask you not to lean on that wall, sir," the doorman said testily.

It was too much for Al. "Sweet Mother of Mary, what in the devil is wrong with ya'?"

"I'm going to call the police now."

"Don't think so," Benny said, coming out of the entrance door. "He's with me. Now you listen, and you listen good. Don't ever trouble this man again. Don't talk to him, don't even look at him. He's a good friend of mine and a very important man. Do you understand?"

The doorman crossed his arms and crinkled his mouth. "I'm just attempting to do my job, sir."

"Well, it was a terrible attempt," Benny said, then cracked a smile. "Think you need to get yourself a woman, relax a bit. Or get rid of a stressful woman, as the case may be."

Al laughed and slapped Benny on the back as they made their way inside. "Great to see ya', Benny."

"Likewise, Al," Benny said, grabbing one of Al's bags and leaning down to give Red a pat. "Wish it could be under better circumstances, but we already know all about this type of lifestyle." He winked. "But I did hear that you had a great funeral."

They crossed the marble floor towards the sleek glass elevator, rolling Al's suitcases behind them.

"That I did," Al said with a grin. "Tragic boat accident. Such a shame. Had a whole wonderful retirement aheada' me."

As they got into the elevator, Al studied Benny's body language carefully. He was almost 100% sure he could trust him, since Benny was the one who had tipped him off. But they had certainly had their ups and downs over the years, and one tiny part of Al wondered if this wasn't some elaborate trap and he was going upstairs to meet his death. It was in moments like these that he half-wished he still wore a bulletproof vest and a had a handgun in his waist.

When they were in the apartment, which was beautiful and sleek, but didn't have much of a view, being on the 4th floor, he had a much more pleasant surprise.

"Joey! Little Fingers!" Al said. "The Gambinos!"

Benny grinned. "A little surprise for you."

They were old friends from his Mafia days. Little Fingers was the son of Fingers, who recruited Al when he was a kid. Even though Little Fingers was now a grown man with a family of his own, the moniker, borne because of his exact likeness to his dad, had stuck.

"Al!" Little Fingers said, giving him a firm handshake and then embracing him in a bear hug. Joey did the same, and Al felt tears springing up in his eyes. He'd felt so alone in the cab ride to the apartment, and now he was surrounded by his best friends in the world.

"Ha-ha, he's crying!" Little Fingers said affectionately, slapping Al on the back. "Now, we've got some of the best champagne to toast your arrival, so hurry up and get them bags put away. Is it okay if I pet your scary lookin' dog?"

"Yeah, if I say it's okay." He turned to Red and said, "It's okay, Red. These are friends."

As if the big Doberman pinscher understood exactly what Al had said, he walked over to Little Fingers and stood in front of him while he bent down and petted Red.

"Your bedroom's over there," Benny said, pointing to a door off the side of the living space.

Al wheeled both his suitcases across the room, still feeling a little jumpy, which was unlike him. He half-expected a gunman to leap out of the closet as soon as he got in the room. Then he caught sight of his worried face in one of the mirrors and gave himself a little slap in the face. "Come on, Al, Man up," he muttered to himself.

Moments later he strode back into the living space. "Guys, that champagne better be the best money can buy! After all, I might jes' get my head blown off in the next coupla' weeks, right?!" He laughed heartily, and the others laughed along, too.

"Nah," Joey said. "Don't even think that way." He passed Al a glass of champagne, the foam overflowing.

Al took it and drained it in one gulp. He held it out to Little Fingers who had the bottle. "Gimme' another one."

"Woohoo," Little Fingers said. "That's the old Al I know."

Al was too full of wired energy to sit down. "Right, so any ideas on who's gunnin' fer me? I'm guessin' it's gotta be the ones behind this recent killin' spree, endin' up with Shirley Morris."

"Ain't got a clue, Al," Benny said. "List could be long as your arm."

"Yeah, figured as much," Al said. "I never even met Shirley Morris. Nothin' really springs to mind. Ya' guys are gonna' need to make some inquiries fer me."

"Of course," Little Fingers and Joey both said. "Field's wide open right now, though. Can't even think of anyone who'd have it in for you and Shirley," Joey said. "It might be a long-held grudge thing. Who knows?"

"I'm thinkin' we gotta' narrow down the connection between

Shirley, them two dead guys, and me," Al said. "Ya' know, work out who mighta' had a grudge against me and them. The way I see it, that's the only way we're gonna' find our killer."

CHAPTER FIVE

Betty Traxel wasn't a bit glamorous, and she could care less. In fact, she liked it that way. She didn't like fancy clothes, makeup, purses, or salons. She thought those were all markers of inferior women with no backbone who only wanted to please men. Her long fuzzy black hair was always tied in a low ponytail, and she wore black velvet suits to work every day.

But there was one thing Betty Traxel loved when it came to her appearance – gold. She had two gold front teeth and wore many gold necklaces, all at once. Her fingers were studded with thick gold rings. She preferred how men's rings looked, and she wore a gold Rolex.

The truth was, if someone looking like her turned up at her restaurant door, she'd never let them in. Unless they were willing to pay their way, of course. Her restaurant, Bella Rosa, was a playground for anyone who had enough money. She rented out the back room for thousands of dollars so people could play poker and have meetings about shady business deals. She always counted the heads that went in, and sometimes one was missing on the way back out.

When anyone asked for the back door key that led to a dark secluded alleyway behind the restaurant, she knew very well what was going on. Body bags were involved. She charged an exorbitant fee for that kind of business and always gave a stern warning that nothing was to come back to her. "The last thing I need is having some pigs dressed in blue come in here and start sniffin' around." And they never did.

It was a good thing, because she carried on a very successful cocaine trade, both in her restaurant and out of it. She sold cocaine by measures of ten kilograms at a time and no less. What anyone did with it after that was their business, but she knew that a lot of the powder and crack circulating in the streets and clubs of Chicago had passed through her hands.

Her nickname was 'The Cook,' and many thought that was because she was the crack cocaine empress of Chicago. The name had stuck, but it had been over fifteen years since she'd cooked up a pot. The name was really about the restaurant which she had bought and furnished with money from her cocaine business.

Betty rarely came out to the front of the restaurant. She wasn't interested in the day-to-day logistics of running her restaurant. Instead, she sat in the back office, doing paperwork, and cutting deals for the drugs and the use of her back room. She kept a close eye on all the finances involved in running the restaurant and other businesses after a bad experience many years ago.

When she found out that her accountant had run off with hundreds of thousands of dollars, she never trusted anyone else to keep track of her finances, afraid they'd dip their hand in the till, just like her accountant had done years ago.

Accountants aren't rich, she thought. They can't see all these millions pouring into my account without getting a case of the green eye. Besides, she enjoyed it. She stayed holed up in the office eating a combination of M&Ms and fancy food from her restaurant, and drinking various combinations of Diet Coke and the finest liqueurs money could buy. She particularly enjoyed chocolate liqueur.

One day, while Betty was working on her accounts, someone barged into her office without knocking. Everyone knew not to enter her office unless they had been summoned by her. She shot up from her desk and reached for her gun, ready to shoot. Then she burst out laughing. "Sam! My god, you gave me a scare!"

Sam, her old friend from school days in inner-city Chicago, a gangly man with a shock of dark hair, edged into the room, laughing nervously. "Don't blow me away, Betty."

"Sit down, you big coward," she said affectionately. "What brings you over here? Not in any trouble, I hope."

"Naw," he said. "Just wanted to pick up some white. Wanted to see if you'd lend me some 'cuz things are slow right now."

Betty paused. She never lent anyone cocaine, because she wasn't prepared to go blasting people's heads off if they didn't pay up. She could get some of the boys to go do it for her, but in Betty's mind, the cleaner her business was, the better. "All right," she said. "But only because it's you. And just a few kilograms."

"You're a gem, Betty," he said.

"Lock the door," she said. "I'll bring it out for you."

When he'd locked it, she crawled under her desk. The coke was in a secret compartment in the floor, each brick weighing a kilogram. She pulled out three of them, then, feeling generous, pulled out an extra one. She and Sam had had a great history. He'd comforted her broken heart fifteen years earlier, though not even his love and support had been enough to fix it. She still felt like there was a wound in her chest, and she'd never considered getting into a relationship with a man since Tommaso.

"Here ya' go," she said, sitting back down and pushing the bricks that were wrapped in paper across her desk. "Put them away."

"Thanks, Betty," he said. "I owe you big time."

"Naw," she said. "You just owe me what it's worth at this level. You'll make a nice profit on that, Sam, 'specially if you break it up small enough."

"And do some mixing," Sam said with a wink.

"That's none of my business," Betty said, holding her hands up. "Don't make it mine."

"All right, all right," Sam said, putting the cocaine in a small leather satchel he'd brought with him. "So, you hear what happened to Shirley Morris?"

"Naw," said Betty. She made a point of staying out of circles of gossip, even Mafia ones. She just pocketed her money and looked the other way. But this piqued her interest. "Why, what happened?"

"Someone took her out," Sam said.

"What? Really?"

"Tried to make it look like suicide. She had hairdressing scissors stabbed in her chest and a suicide note saying she was guilty for killing all of her husbands." His voice became quiet and his eyes were intense. "Whad'ya think about that?"

Betty felt an old heart-wrenching feeling in her chest, one that she'd felt for so many years. Not only had Shirley taken Tommaso, she'd murdered him in cold blood, too. She'd always denied it, but most everyone believed she was responsible for his death.

"I don't know what to say," Betty said. "I mean, I'm glad that nasty murdering b-word is off the face of this planet. Someone had to do it, and as far as I'm concerned, they ought to get a medal for doing it."

"Right," Sam said.

"But... it doesn't bring Tommaso back," Betty mumbled more to herself than to Sam.

"You're right about that," Sam said. "It's been a long time, though, Bet. Don't you think you could..."

"Don't you dare give me any crap about moving on, Sam," Betty said, pointing her finger at him, flaming rage flying from her eyes.

"Aw, come on, Betty, I was just saying…"

"Well, you can just not say," she said. She started looking back over her accounts and furiously typed numbers into her computer, although her mind was beginning to fuzz over, as it did whenever she thought of Tommaso. "Look, I'm just glad she's gone, although I wouldn't want to be where she is, but she deserves it. Now, I'm perfectly happy with my life. You come here to borrow some coke, or to be my therapist?"

Sam sighed. "You're such a hard piece of work."

"Well, why are you here, then? Get out if all you're gonna' do is come here and talk trash at me. In fact, give me back that cocaine. Come on. Come on!"

"Betty, don't be like this," Sam said. "I thought you'd gotten over that rage a long time ago."

"Fine. Keep it. Whatever. See if I care. Four keys ain't nothing to me, anyways, Sam, as you well know. And why are you down and out? Why did you have to come here and beg me for some free stuff, huh? If you've got your life together so well, why don't you have enough for your coke? Maybe my rage is serving me well, ya' think?"

She laid her hands out on the desk, ostentatiously showing off her rings. She wiggled her pinky finger, which had a huge diamond on it. "This ring is worth ten times more than my goods you've got in your bag. Who has their life together now, huh, Sam?"

"Whatever, Betty," Sam said. He crossed one leg over the other in a nonchalant way and lit up a cigarette. "I hate you when you're like this."

"I hate you at all times," she countered.

Sam lifted the corners of his mouth in a smile, a look so infuriating it made Betty laugh.

"Just leave me alone!" she shouted at him, but a modest smile was tugging at her lips.

Sam burst out laughing. "You really do love me, Betty. I'm the only person in the world who isn't afraid of you. That's gotta' count for something, right?"

She tried to go back to her accounts. "You're a fool, Sam."

"So are you. Two crazy fools together," he said. "Me, having made millions and lost it all. And you, heartbroken over a man who left you fifteen years ago and died ten years ago. We're kind of ridiculous, aren't we?"

Despite the burn in her chest, Betty could see his point. "Maybe. Want some liqueur? I sure do."

"Yeah, sure," he said. He picked up a bottle sitting on the corner of her desk. "Chocolate liqueur. Isn't that a bit girly?"

She grinned, and poured two glasses. "Perfect for you, then."

"Thanks," he said, pretending to be outraged.

"Naw, you'd better not have anything stronger. Not sure you could take it after the first sip. She pushed the glass toward him. "You idiot."

Sam lifted the glass. "Cheers to two crazy, ridiculous, stupid people."

"Well, you'll be on your own with that one," Betty said. "I'm totally sane, filthy rich, and have an IQ that can run rings around Einstein's."

"You should be more confident of your abilities," Sam said

sarcastically.

Betty rolled her eyes. "What else do you want, or are you finally going to get out of my office?" She wanted him to stay, but Betty rarely did what she really wanted to do. She did what had to be done, and she didn't want to go soft.

Sam laughed. "You're still the same. Only a little fatter and a little more bitter."

Betty made a little bow towards him. "Thanks, Sam. You're still the same. Only a little poorer and a ton more pathetic."

"Ouch," Sam said.

Betty clinked her glass with his and took a huge swig of the liqueur. Then she lit a cigar and grinned at him. "Don't dish out what you can't take."

"I guess you're right," Sam said. "Now… honestly…" He shifted in his chair, and it was the first time he'd looked uncomfortable since he'd come into her office. "I want to ask you a question."

"Will I marry you? Sorry, no, babe. You're gay, accept it, and I'm not gonna be your beard."

"I'm serious, Betty."

"Spit it out, then."

"Did you… well, I was wondering… I mean, I guess you—"

"Oh, come on, Sam, spit it out!"

"Okay," Sam said. He took a deep breath. "I'll just ask you straight out. Did you kill Shirley?"

There was a long silence while they just stared at each other.

"No," Betty said, looking away from him. "Maybe I should have, but I didn't."

"Are you telling me the truth?" he asked. "Swear to it?"

"I don't have to swear anything to you," Betty said. "Have you forgotten who I am? Just because we were friends a long time ago doesn't mean you have a free pass to come in here and disrespect me. You know what would happen to anyone else if they talked to me like you're doing now?"

"I'm not everyone else," Sam said. "And I'm not disrespecting you. It was just a question."

"And that was just my answer."

Sam grinned at her. "It's like we were kids again. Same old arguments."

But Betty wasn't in the mood for that anymore. "Look, Sam, you got what you wanted. Can you just go, please?" It was so confusing being around him. She hated it and loved it at the same time. She felt she could open up to him, like she did to no one else in the world. But there was something intimidating about the intimacy.

Everyone else feared her, and it created a wonderful distance between them that meant she could run away from every difficult conversation and every awkward moment she ever encountered.

Everything could be covered up with a stern face and barking and yelling. But Sam wasn't fazed by any of it. He wasn't remotely scared of her. It was exhilarating and exhausting, both at once.

"Yeah, sure," he said, getting up. "Call me anytime."

"You're darn right I will," she said. "You owe me money for what's in your bag. You're lucky I let you keep it."

"You'll see that money real soon," he said. "See you, Betty."

"Yeah, right, you're a failure at life, Sam," she said, just before he went out the door. Then, when the door had clicked closed, she felt guilty. "Bye, buddy," she said, even though he was already gone. The office felt so much lonelier after he left.

CHAPTER SIX

Rocco Rosetti, also known as The Rock, was one of Chicago's most feared gangsters. There were two reasons for this. One, because he had no family, and this made him reckless, and two, because he looked absolutely terrifying. At 6'7" he was extremely tall. He also had a huge scar running from his right ear to the right corner of his mouth. This was known as a 'snitch cut', being in the shape of a phone, and was doled out to those who ran to the police.

The truth was, Rocco had once been an informer. A cop had offered him a boatload of cash to feed him information, so he thought, Why not? He didn't owe anyone loyalty. He had no family to think about or consider. He'd been betrayed in the business more times than he could count. Why shouldn't he put himself first for once?

His height and his scar were terrifying. In addition to that were his piercing blue eyes that had a wild intensity about them and made people stop in their tracks. Some women, insane ones, found him irresistibly attractive. Others wanted to run away at the very sight of him. He had a polarizing effect on just about everyone he came across.

Currently, he was holed up in a woman's apartment and had been for the last three days. They'd lost themselves in a drug-filled haze, which had come to be the only way he could deal with life. He'd murdered too many people. Sometimes he had nightmares about them, their dead open eyes staring up at him from their death-place on the ground.

That was how he'd lived his life for the past eighteen months, bouncing around drug addicted women's apartments, leaving whenever they sparked his rage, and he began to feel murderous. He really tried not to murder women if it was at all avoidable.

This one, nicknamed Foxie, wasn't too bad. She was docile, meek, and pliable, and as long as he would provide her with heroin, she'd do whatever he said. She was a pretty good cook, too, and he made her cook him up meals every single day without fail. His favorite was a steak she made with a red wine mushroom sauce that he thought was the best thing he'd ever eaten. Just thinking about it made his mouth water.

She rubbed his feet, stroked his hair, and let him make love to her whenever he wanted. Whenever he got into a rage, she cowered in the corner and cried. That always made him angry, but once he'd hit her, he felt much better. Then she'd give him a big hug, and he'd calm down. He thought he'd probably stay around for as long as he could.

That particular day, Foxie was in a happy mood and was dancing around the rundown apartment in her underwear. She said, "So when are we going to get that luxury apartment, babe?"

Rocco had filled her head with all sorts of stories. The truth was, he had had a luxury apartment at one time, when business was going well. But just when things were going smoothly for Rocco, it all felt wrong. He had this terrible cloud hanging over his head, like something was going to go really bad. Instead of waiting for the impending doom to happen, each time he'd destroy his life on his own terms.

When he had money, he gambled it all away and didn't pay the rent. The landlords came after him, and he threatened that he'd slit their throat if they ever came asking for rent again. They said they'd send the police over, and since he was high on cocaine and up to his neck in criminality, he thought it was probably better not to have a little tea party with Chicago's finest officers. He was out of that apartment like a lightning bolt, but of course he trashed it before he left. He smashed all the mirrors on the floor, broke a window, and poured red wine over the pristine white carpet.

He'd lied to Foxie and said that all his crime proceeds were locked up in a Swiss bank account, to the tune of $30 million. He was just waiting for his lawyer to help him get the money out. This was the story he rolled out every time he asked her for a measly $10 here or there. She sold her body out on the street to buy drugs sometimes. Other times, he went out and robbed a drug dealer or two, to cover their expenses.

"I don't know, babe," he replied, sprawling out on the couch. "But when that money comes, we can buy five apartments. We'll live in one, rent out four, and live a life of total luxury. Just wait and see, babe. We'll be like celebrities."

She jumped on the couch next to him, full of excitement, and tucked her legs up under her. Her eyes were bright with wonder. "Ooh, babe, can I have a Rolls Royce?"

"Of course you can," he said. "That's nothing. You can have seven Rolls Royces if you want, one for each day of the week."

"And Gucci bags? And Louis Vuitton outfits? And can we drink the finest wine?"

"We'll be drinking it for breakfast out of mugs, darling," he said. "Now give me $10. I want to go buy some crackers and cheese. In fact, you go buy them. Put some clothes on, and hurry up. Come right back here. I don't want any man to steal you away from me."

The truth was, no one was even remotely likely to steal Foxie. She was dangerously underweight, was missing a front tooth, and had acne all over her face from her drug use.

As soon as Foxie left, Rocco rushed to her jar in the kitchen where she kept her money from turning tricks. He emptied it out - $32 - and slipped it in his pocket. She'd wonder where it was when she returned, but he'd just convince her she'd already spent it. Over the years, he'd become adept at mind games, and was a master liar and manipulator.

When she returned, she went in the kitchen and began to fix his crackers and cheese without being asked. He had her well-trained. Soon she returned with them on a plate, along with a glass of juice. "Eat up, Rocco," she said. "You know, when I was at the store, I saw on the news something about this hairdresser woman. She was found with her hairdressing scissors pierced through her chest. Can you believe that?"

He shrugged and stuffed a cracker into his mouth. "So what?"

"Don't you think that sounds horrible? I mean, poor woman."

"She wouldn't feel sorry for you."

"What? Do you know her?"

"No."

"So why did you say that?"

He looked up at her with murder in his eyes. "Are you asking me questions?" he said in a low tone of voice that pierced through the air between them.

"No, no, sorry, babe, I'm not." She sat next to him and cuddled into his arm. He pushed her away, but then she did it again and he allowed her to stay. "Sorry, baby. I'm really sorry. Please don't be angry with me."

He began to feel the rage rising in him. Who was she to question him, this pathetic drug addict that no one would want? He only wanted her for a place to rest his head. He stared at the TV, well, through the TV really, because he couldn't focus. He chomped on his crackers and cheese, feeling anger pumping in his chest.

"Babe," Foxie asked, in a squeaky mouse-like voice. "Are you okay?"

He leaped to his feet, grabbed the plate, and threw it at the opposite wall. It smashed in pieces onto the floor. "Shut up!" he roared at her. He hated anyone asking him if he was all right. "I can't stand the sight of you." He stormed out into the hallway and ran down the stairway that smelled of drugs, trash and urine.

Rocco walked a block over to the bar that had a slot machine. He bought one drink at the bar and changed the rest of the money into dollar bills to gamble. Half of him wanted to win - $100 was the jackpot - and the other half of him wanted to lose. If he won, he'd likely just put it all back in the machine and lose it again, anyway. When you had no plans for your life, what was the use of money?

Rocco nursed his whiskey – which Foxie had begged him not to drink, because it made him even more violent than usual – and pushed dollar after dollar into the slot machine. Sitting in front of the machine, he pulled the lever. No match. And again. No match. Dollar after dollar turned into loss after loss, and in less than two minutes, all his money was gone.

He stared at the machine, wondering what to do next. He was beginning to think perhaps he should have bought some food, because his belly was rumbling and the crackers hadn't made much inroad into his hunger. Or maybe he should have bought the next hit, so he and Foxie could get high and forget the world. He was beginning to feel flat and uncomfortable. The inevitable comedown.

"Hey man," someone said from behind him. Rocco flinched and turned. "Are you using the machine?"

Rocco looked up at the guy from where he was seated. The man was a short dark-haired man who looked like he worked out. Rocco studied him for a moment. "Who's asking?"

The short man laughed and said, "Do you own this machine, brother? Come on, man, let an old guy take a try."

Rocco got up very slowly from the seat, watching the man all the while, and then shifted into the seat next to the machine.

"Looks like I've got an audience!" the short man said cheerfully, sitting down. "Well, you're not in for much of a show. I've only got $2 to spin." The man pushed in his first dollar, and Rocco watched intently. The man pulled the lever, and the pictures on the slot machine began to spin, but when they stopped, none of them matched.

"Bad luck," Rocco said, smirking at him.

The man pushed the next dollar into the machine, then pulled the lever. First, a 7 came up. Rocco held his breath. Then came another 7. And finally, another 7. The machine went wild, with flashing lights and music, and proceeded to spit out five crisp new $20 bills. The short man jumped off the stool, threw his hands in the air, and said, "Yes!" Then he grabbed Rocco to hug him.

Rocco, incensed, pushed him away so hard the man fell on the floor. Then Rocco scooped all the money out of the machine before the man could get back up. "Thank you!" he said.

The man had gotten up and his face was turning red. "That's my money!" he said angrily. "Give it back!" He threw himself at Rocco, but Rocco was faster. He grabbed his glass and smashed it over the man's head. Blood began to spurt out from the top of the man's head and some flew in his face. He tasted it on his tongue.

By now, the bar crowd had erupted. Two men grabbed Rocco from behind.

"What do you think you're doing?" the short man said, his hands covered in blood from where he'd touched his head. "You're psycho! Keep the money, if it means that much to you. You're a maniac!"

"Good!" Rocco yelled, straining against the men who held him back. "You're lucky I didn't kill you like I killed that cop!"

CHAPTER SEVEN

Donald Richards, better known as Porky, sat by the pool in the back yard of his Miami mansion, sipping on rosé wine. His big belly made him look pregnant, and his long black hair, which he coiled into a neat braid down his back, made him look more like a grotesque kind of woman than a man. He wore fluorescent yellow speedos that showed everybody far more than they wanted to see.

His business manager Edwin, an African American Florida native, who was not connected to the Mafia, sweated beside him on a chaise lounge, dressed in a suit and tie. Porky always made a point of being casual while insisting that everyone else follow strict codes of formality. It was his way of keeping them in check and showing them who was the boss.

He was glad to be out of the Mafia, where strict family codes and hierarchies kept him in his place. Here? His aggression and money were enough to put him at the head of the pack, and he wasn't going to give up that status for anyone. Back in Chicago, he'd gotten tired of always having to answer to the higher-ups.

That was why they'd put the hit on him in the first place. He'd once been married to Shirley Morris, the 'Black Widow' who had left a trail of dead husbands in her wake. He was the third, and he'd thought she'd just had terrible luck with her first two spouses. The first had been hit by a car, and the second had some extreme form of food poisoning that left him in a coma for a few days before he passed away.

Naturally, being a mobster, he was initially suspicious of Shirley. But she'd seemed so genuine, both about her sorrow over the deaths of her previous husbands, and about her true love for Porky. She was a great actress.

That said, he'd still kept a slightly suspicious eye on her. He'd been inducted into the Mafia by his father when he was twelve and had been around long enough to know not everything was as it seemed. To that end, he'd installed a keystroke detector on her computer, and a tracker on her phone, which she knew nothing about. He'd tried to install a camera system in her salon, but getting it all set up without her knowing proved to be too difficult.

"Sir, that Ortega guy just isn't budging on the property deal," Edwin said. "The rest of the board is in favor of making the sale. Only Ortega is holding everything back. What shall we do, sir?"

Porky sniffed. "Get rid of him."

Edwin shifted on the chaise lounge, not sure if he was more uncomfortable from sweating in his suit or being asked to arrange a hit. "I'm sorry, sir, I don't know what you mean."

Porky took a sip of his rosé, and said, "You know very well what I mean."

Edwin said, "Sir, you can't mean…?" He trailed off.

Porky launched his bulk off of his chaise lounge, lunged forward, and grabbed Edwin by the scruff of the neck. "Kill him, you idiot. You've arranged this kind of thing once before. You mean to tell me you can't do it again?"

Edwin looked at the ground. "Sir, I don't know if you remember, but I mentioned that I wasn't really comfortable with that sort of thing last time, and you told me that we weren't going to do it again."

Porky pushed his sunglasses on top of his head and looked Edwin in the eye. "You know what could happen to this company if this deal doesn't go through?"

"No, sir. I can't see any potential ramifications."

"You're blind. We'd lose our reputation. Listen to this, Edwin. We've been doing property deals for less than five years, and already we're flipping commercial buildings to the tune of hundreds of millions. I've never lost a single deal, and I don't plan to start now. Do you want to be the man to encourage me to start losing?"

"Of course not, sir. I just... well... isn't there another way to do it? Maybe we should bring Ortega here for a meeting?"

"Wonderful idea," Porky said. "Then you can shoot him and push him in the pool." He laughed raucously. "Just kidding. Don't ever think of killing anyone here."

"I wouldn't think of killing anyone ever," Edwin said. "I'm just taking your orders. But in all honesty, sir, I might have to reconsider my position with you. I didn't sign up to organize murders."

"Too late," Porky said. "You're stuck with me for life now. You've killed already, and you have no proof that I asked you to do it. You're as guilty as I am, and you're sticking by me to the end. Tell you what, Edwin, boy. Get Ortega out the way permanently, make sure this deal goes through, tie up all the paperwork and the deals, and I'll make you CEO.

"I'll even toss in a new Bentley or a Porsche or an Aston Martin, whatever you want. Arrange the hit now, go home, take the weekend off, and go car shopping with your wife. Sound good?" He didn't wait for a response as he gave Edwin a hard slap on the back. "There. That's a good boy. Off you go."

Edwin left without another word, looking intensely stressed.

Porky laid back on the lounge again, feeling more worried than he looked. In all his years in the Mafia, he'd learned to hide his emotions very well. He was a little concerned about the Ortega hit. When he'd come to Miami, he'd vowed to get into the real estate business and be as lily clean as Mother Theresa.

He wouldn't do any hits, and he wouldn't cheat or swindle anyone. Perhaps he'd even find himself a good woman to make his wife, and he'd finally become an upstanding family man. He could even find a Catholic church and become a lay deacon.

But that hadn't worked out. He'd found the real estate game was much messier and shadier than he'd anticipated. All the women he met appeared to be gold diggers. He had a girlfriend back in Chicago, and he decided maybe he'd get serious with her instead of looking for someone new.

The one thing he did find was a good church, but he'd committed so many sins during his life, he finally realized he'd never be considered for becoming a lay deacon. He'd stopped going to church a couple of years ago.

He thought it was pretty ironic that even though he was hundreds of miles away from Chicago and the mob life he'd left behind, he'd fallen into an industry just as dangerous and corrupt, where people still died in mysterious circumstances.

Given that, when he bought his estate, he'd added a huge perimeter wall around the whole ten-acre property, even though it cost amounts so big it made his head hurt. He also built a few guard stations around the perimeter where hired security lurked at all hours of the day and night, with dogs and guns at the ready.

He'd never felt safe after what had happened with Shirley Morris.

His phone, which was lying under his chaise lounge, buzzed. He strained around his big belly to pick it up. He looked at the screen. The screen read The Cook.

"Betty," he said, overjoyed. "I'm so glad to hear from you!" They knew each other from his mob days back in Chicago, where he used to rent her back room to play poker and take care of other business-related issues.

"You hear what happened to Shirley? Are you that out of the loop now?"

"Yeah, I heard about it. Too bad for her," he said. "Finally, all her wrongdoings have caught up with her. What am I supposed to do, cry about it? The woman wanted to kill me, for heaven's sake. If it hadn't been for you overhearing one of her conversations concerning me and tipping me off, I'd be dead as a doornail right now."

"I'd trade you for Tommaso in a heartbeat," Betty said. "If I had to kill you to bring him back, you better believe I would."

"I'm sorry about Tommaso, Betty," he said. "I know how it feels to lose people close to you. So how did she die?"

Betty told him about the scissors and the suicide note, and said that everyone knew it really was a hit. "The cops are staying out of it. They know it's Mafia business."

"You think she was a rat?"

"Naw," Betty said. "Well, maybe. I don't know. She certainly left a trail of bodies in her wake. There are a lot of people who would have happily rammed those scissors into her chest."

"You and me included, right?" Porky said.

"Right," Betty said. "I didn't, though."

"Neither did I," he said. "I haven't got time for settling past issues. I'm thinking about the future." The sun was starting to feel hot on Porky's big belly, so he got up, pushed his fat feet into his slider sandals, and padded across the tiles to the shaded flower garden. "So, talking about the future. What are your plans? Still doing a roaring trade of the white?"

"You bet I am," Betty said. "And my back room is still in business."

"Good."

Betty laughed. "I thought you were going to give me a lecture. Tell me to go straight, to get out of the game, like you."

"Well, we do what we have to, don't we, Betty? It was my time to get out. Maybe your time will come."

Betty laughed again. "I just hope I don't get smoked first."

"I'd be willing to bet you wouldn't let anyone get close enough to you to do that," he said.

"That's true. You keep your circle tight, and I keep mine non-existent. Anyways, I've gotta' go and do some accounts. Take care, Porky."

"Unfortunately, Betty, I have the misfortune of having to come to Chicago on some business in a couple of days. They're having problems at one of my businesses, and I have to check it out. We'll have to do dinner."

"Okay. Sounds good. See you soon, Porky."

CHAPTER EIGHT

Al decided the best course of action for him to take was to go see Shirley's daughter. Little Fingers was the one who shot out the idea over lunch the day after Al arrived. Al, Little Fingers, and Benny (Joey had some business to take care of) sat in the glass-walled apartment, looking out at the city, and Al was uneasy. He had these visions of snipers hiding on the roof of a nearby building, ready to burst a bullet through the glass.

Benny must have seen him looking around nervously, because he said, "That glass is bulletproof, by the way. That was something I asked 'em about before I booked it for you. They gave me a funny look, I can tell you. I just pretended to be a nervous guy who was afraid of bomb blasts and terrorist attacks, heck, even his own shadow."

Al shook his head. "Benny, ya' shoulda' been an actor."

Benny winked. "Maybe I'd aspire to be one, except for the fact I make about ten times what they do."

Al couldn't concentrate on Benny's banter. "So where am I gonna' find her? Shirley's daughter?" he asked Little Fingers.

"Um… she's just had a baby. She's married to Saul Russo. Her name is Angelina. She'll probably be at home."

"Saul Russo… Saul Russo… Name rings a bell."

"Saul was a fixer few years back. Died of a heart attack. Think that was real, to be honest. He always stuffed himself full of red meat," Benny said. "This is really Saul Russo Jr., but everyone calls him Saul. He's young, about twenty-three, I'd say. His father had him late in life."

"Oh, yeah," Al said. "Think I remember the ol' guy. Had a crooked eye, right?"

"You got it," Little Fingers said. "I had to drop off a package there one time. I don't remember the house, but I remember the neighborhood. They shouldn't be hard to find."

Al shuddered involuntarily. "Ima gonna' make it work," he said, but his voice lacked conviction. "Seems like everyone's somehow connected in this sorry saga. Jes' hope they don't tip off whoever's lookin' for me."

"You're not going soft, are ya'?" Benny asked, poking him with the round end of his fork and laughing.

"No way," Al said, shoving Benny by the shoulder in a joking way. "Bite thy tongue."

Once he'd washed down all his chicken and potatoes with copious amounts of white wine, Al got a cab to the street Little Fingers had mentioned. He decided his best bet was to walk a little ways away from the apartment building and catch the first cab that came by.

He didn't want to call a cab firm from the apartment, in case the phone had been tampered with. There were some scam masters around who could reroute any phone number sent to their own, and pretended to be banks, police, FBI, just about anybody. He had no idea who was trying to kill him, but if they were high enough up in the mob hierarchy, they could very well have control over that kind of technology.

It wasn't a long ride to the street where Angelina and Saul Russo's home was located. They lived in a large three-story house, on a row of other homes that were all the same. It was clearly an upscale street, and the driveways in front of the homes were filled with BMWs, Mercedes, and Jaguars.

Al paid the cab driver, then stepped out onto the street, looking up and down at each house. He realized there was absolutely no way to tell where Angelina lived. He took a deep breath, willing her to come out the front door of her home with a stroller, but she didn't.

Al wasn't one to turn back, so he marched up to a random house and knocked on the front door. After a few moments an old man opened the door. "Good afternoon, sir," Al said. "Ima lookin' for Angelina and Saul Russo. I heard they live…"

"Oh, them," the old man said, spitting the words out with disapproval. "Yeah, they live at the last house down the street in this development. Think it's number 18."

He was closing the door when Al said, "Excuse me, but it seems you dislike them people. Mind tellin' me why?"

The old man wrinkled his nose. "I'm sure they're drug dealers. There are shady characters in fancy cars coming and going from their house at all times of the day and night. Mostly I mind my own business, but there's a child in there. That's no environment for a child. I should report them to child protective services. I will, when I get enough evidence."

He looked Al up and down, as if realizing he'd said too much. "Well, I probably won't, but, well, you know…"

"Okay. Thanks fer the directions."

"Yeah."

Al walked down to the end of the street, and sure enough, there was number 18. All the things the old man said played in his mind –

all the shady characters coming and going. He really wished he was armed. All he could hope for was that he didn't wander in on a meeting.

He checked his phone to make sure it was on, and that he could get in touch with Benny quickly if he needed to. Then he took a deep breath and knocked on the door.

Less than a minute later, he was met with the sight of a young woman in a sweatsuit, holding a baby in her arms. She had dark rings under her eyes. "You here to see Saul?" she asked in a tired voice.

"Hi there," Al said. "No, actually I'm here to see ya'."

"Me?" Her eyes narrowed. She was clearly suspicious of him. Al felt sad, in a way. Such a young woman, already suspicious and worried by being around too many Mafia characters.

"Yeah," he said. "I wanna' talk to ya' 'bout your mother."

She stepped back defensively. "Who are you? You're not a cop, are you?"

"No," he said. He tried to read the situation and then made a snap decision that telling the truth would be best. He lowered his voice. "Look, someone's after me. I think it might be the same person who got yer' mother. I wanna' find out who killed her and hopefully get 'em brought to justice, so they can't do the same to me."

She sighed wearily. "You've got one heck of a job on your hands."

"I know," he said. "Used to be in the mob, but I retired and tried to build a new life. Lotta' people don't like that I was able to do that."

"I know exactly what you mean," she said. "I want to… Well, I just met you. How can I tell you that? But I want to get out. Sometimes I wish I could just take a plane to Europe and never see a single Mafia face again."

Al laughed a little sadly. "Trust me, I know the feelin'. Listen, I'm really sorry about yer' mother."

Angelina shook her head. "Thanks. It's been hard. Some people say she deserved it. She was no angel. I've known that from the time I was a little girl." The baby whined a little, and she bounced him to make him settle down. "I want something different for my boy. I don't know how many Mafia mothers I've seen that had to bury their sons. I don't want to do that."

Al nodded. "Hopefully ya' can get out."

Her eyes clouded with sadness. "I don't know. Saul says he's enjoying it."

"I was once a young man in the business, jes' like him. He's probably caught up in the drama and excitement of it all."

"Yes," Angelina said, starting to sound angry. "How well I know that. Before Hudson was born, I didn't mind. But now… well, it all seems so empty and immature."

"You're a wise young woman, Angelina," Al said. "Not many see that 'til it's too late. I hope ya' can get out soon, but it might hafta' be without Saul."

The defensive look on her face let him know he'd gone a step too far. "And you are?" she said.

"Oh, sorry, my name is Al."

"Al…?"

"Al De Duco."

"Nice to meet you, Al. Now I have to go take care of my baby."

"Wait, wait, jes' a second," Al said. "I jes' wanted to ask you if anyone was botherin' your mother before she died?"

Someone shouted angrily from inside. "Angelina!"

A worried look spread across her face. "Sorry, sorry," she said quickly. "I have to go…"

Al thought quickly. "Let's meet somewhere to talk."

He could see the cogs whirring in her brain as she began to shut the door. "Fine. In two hours, the coffee shop on the main street, around the corner. Gina's. Goodbye."

She quickly shut the door, and Al had a feeling he should rush away from the house as soon as possible. He hurried around the corner, out of sight of the house. Then he heard the sound of running footsteps coming from behind him.

Al hadn't lasted in the Mafia for so many years being stupid. He turned, facing back the way he had just come from, and began strolling along. He called Benny and tried to look nonchalant.

A young dark-haired man came running around the corner from the street he'd been on, then stopped, looking confused. Al could tell he was Saul, because he looked so much like his father. He had his hand resting on his waist, making it clear he was armed. "Hey!" he said to Al, his voice pumped with aggression. "Were you just talking to my girl?"

Al screwed up his face as if he was confused. "What are you talkin' 'bout? Ya' got the wrong guy. I'm jes' going to see an ol' friend of mine who lives down there." He gestured towards the row of houses around the corner.

Saul clearly didn't know whether to believe him or not. "Right."

Al casually walked past him. As he passed by Saul, he could feel his gaze following him all the way. He guessed there was no alternative except to knock on the old man's door again.

"Oh, you didn't find them?" the old man asked.

"Mattera' fact I did, and I got a li'l too much of 'em," Al said. "If I give ya' $100, would ya' let me come in? I jes' need to stay for five minutes until that guy stops watchin' me."

"What on earth are you involving me in?" the old man asked.

Al looked at him with pleading eyes. "Please."

The old man looked him up and down. "Make it $200."

"Done," Al said immediately.

"If you try any funny business, the police will be here in two minutes. I have an alarm, and I keep it on me at all times."

"Thanks."

The old man stepped aside and let him in. "No funny business, you hear?"

"Absolutely none," Al said. He looked at the door to the left. "Ya' got a window we can look out of, so I can see when this guy's gone?"

"Sure," the old man said. "That's the kitchen. Follow me."

The old man led the way into the kitchen and grabbed a large knife out of a butcher block. He stood in front of it and grinned apologetically. "I still don't know who you are."

"No problem," Al said. "Know how ya' feel." He went over to the window and peered out. Saul was still standing out on the sidewalk.

"Looks like you're mixed up in a whole load of trouble," the old man said.

Al's nose twitched. "Ya' could say that." Finally, after a few minutes, Saul turned and went back into number 18. Al waited for a couple more minutes to make sure he wouldn't come back out, then said, "He's gone. I gotta' go. Here's yer' $200. Thanks a lot."

"You take care now," the old man said. "Don't get yourself killed."

"Ima gonna' try not to," Al said, going back out through the front door. He turned the other way, away from number 18, and hurried down the street.

As he walked, he tapped 'Gina's' into his Google Maps, and got the walking directions. It was only a three-minute walk from where he was, so he made the decision to go on foot. He just hoped he wasn't spotted by anyone. It appeared Saul's place was a Mafia hotspot, and he guessed a lot of mob types would be driving around in the area.

Eventually he got to Gina's, a sleek café decorated in neutrals and browns. It was quite cozy inside, although very modern. He ordered a cappuccino and sat down at the back of the café, where he couldn't be seen from the street. He had a little under two hours to wait, and even then, there was no guarantee that Angelina would or could show up.

Although he was no fan of Shirley's, he did feel sorry for Angelina. She hadn't asked for this life. He couldn't imagine what it must be like to be raised by a Mafia mother who had killed so many husbands, and then married off to a member of the Russo family?

She obviously had grown up in a cage and she was still trapped in it. He got the impression that Saul wasn't exactly a gentle and caring husband. Al wondered if Angelina did try to get away, if Saul was the type to track her down to the ends of the earth, or even kill her.

He wanted to call Cassie. He already missed her, but by now she was in the air with DeeDee and Jake on their way to Chicago. They were due to arrive in the early evening. He couldn't wait to see them. They were part of his new life, the chapter where he was an upstanding regular man, not part of a secret and dangerous underworld organization. He thought about Red and how he was a part of his world. He hoped Red was behaving back at the apartment.

He wished Red was with him for back up, but he knew Red would draw attention and above all, he was trying to avoid that.

Cassie would help him keep his head, and not let him slip back into any of his old Mafia ways because of the pressure he was under. He was very aware of just how easy it would be to let his fear turn into aggression. He was already tense about going to the police. He began to wonder if that really was the best option? His head was exploding with it all.

He decided he needed a break, and logged onto the internet on his phone. There were a few forums he liked to post on. A couple about wine, one about fishing, one about traveling. He tapped onto the latter, and started a thread about where would people suggest he go with Cassie on their next vacation. It helped. It was like declaring to the world that there was no way he was going to die in Chicago. He was planning his next trip for when all of this was over.

Luckily a couple of other members were on, and they got into conversations about Nepal and Bali and New Zealand. He got lost in his own little world of travel plans, completely forgetting about where he was or what he was doing.

"Hello, Al."

He flinched in surprise. His nerves weren't what they once were, and then he looked up. "Oh, hello, Angelina. … Can I get ya' some coffee?"

She was pushing a stroller and was looking more dressed up, with high heels, makeup, and a fur coat. "Thanks, but the barista's bringing it over for me. I don't have long." She sat down beside him. She checked on the baby, who was asleep. "I told Saul I was meeting my girlfriend for coffee. I got one of my friends to lie on the phone to him. He always double checks. But he might come by and peer in the window, so the quicker we get this done, the better. What do you want to know?"

"Was anyone botherin' your mother before she died?"

"People were always bothering her," Angelina said. "It was like that my whole life. I don't know who it was, though. I stopped paying too much attention a long time ago, since nothing had ever happened. I figured they were empty threats. But not this time..." She wiped a tear away.

Al wanted to comfort her, but knew they didn't have time for that. "Okay," he said, thinking fast. "What about at her funeral? Did anyone make a big deal about bein' sad? That's usually a red flag."

"Yeah, one guy did. Think his name was Sab. He's that disfigured guy who got acid thrown in his face. He was crying a lot."

"I know who ya' mean," Al said. Surly Sab was a well-known character, and he didn't like Al. "Okay. Anyone else?"

"No, that's it."

"All right. I don't wanna' jeopardize your safety... or mine. So I'm gonna' go. Oh, and please don't mention me to anyone. Everyone thinks I'm dead, and I'd like to keep it that way fer as long as possible."

"My lips are sealed," Angelina said.

Al hurried out of the coffee shop and hailed a cab.

CHAPTER NINE

"Wow, this is quite a place," DeeDee said, looking out the windows of the apartment. Unfortunately, it wasn't up high enough to see over the whole city, but it was still quite impressive. The apartment itself looked like it had just been built. Everything was shiny and new, and the kitchen was like a little palace all in marble.

"I'll have Benny's head," Al joked. He had his arm around Cassie's waist, holding her close. It was clear he'd missed her, even in the short time they'd been apart. "He shoulda' got me the darn penthouse. Fer a guy full of money, he really is cheap. He's gonna' be here pretty soon. He jes' called me. And, yeah, feel free to tell him I said he's cheap. That'll get in his head and mess with him."

Jake laughed. "This is plenty good enough, Al, don't worry about it. It's clearly a prime piece of real estate."

"It sure is," said Cassie, smiling up at Al with so much love in her eyes, he thought his heart would burst.

"This area's on the up," Al said. "Used to be a lot of ol' rundown housin' projects around here, but they got torn down and replaced with luxury apartments and office buildins'. If I was inclined that way, I'd be pumpin' a ton of money into 'em. Maybe if we were somewhere else I would. But in Chicago? Not a chance! I gots me way too much history here."

"Is it weird to be back, Al?" Deedee asked. "Knowing that your life is so different from the last time you were here?"

"Yeah, I feel like a new man," Al said, "and like I shouldn't be here. But if I gotta' be here, I jes' wanna' get this chapter of my life finished and continue rewritin' my life with absolutely no mob drama in it at all. This is the last time Ima gonna' find myself mixed up in anythin' involvin' the mob. All of ya' can hold ol' Al to that. Ima gonna' make sure the past don't catch up with me again."

"When I'm investigating, I often find murders are committed because of grievances or events that happened way in the past," Jake said. He spoke from experience because he owned a private investigation firm back in the Seattle area. He had temporarily taken over a friend's private investigation firm in Connecticut when his wife became ill and was scheduled to return there within the week. Al had been issued a private investigating license in Washington and was filling in for Jake while he was gone.

"People who were once members of a criminal organization often find that their past comes back to bite them, even when they straighten out," Jake said.

"Jake," DeeDee hissed, disliking his insensitivity towards Al.

"No, DeeDee, what he's sayin' is true," Al said. "Wouldn't mind if it was jes' me, but it's Cassie, too. Sometimes I think she woulda' been better off marryin' someone without a past like mine. You know, someone with a normal background."

Cassie held Al close in a warm and loving embrace. "I wouldn't change you for the world, darling. And I knew all about your past when we got married, so I went into it with my eyes wide open. I didn't expect this to happen, but I love you, I'm committed to you, and I'm here to see this through with you."

Al's eyes lit up as he smiled. He grinned at Jake. "Ima thinkin' I might jes' have the best woman in the world, huh?"

Jake put an arm around DeeDee and said, "I'll give you a run for your money, pal."

They all laughed.

"Lemme' show ya' yer' room," Al said to DeeDee and Jake.

DeeDee and Jake followed him into a wonderfully spacious bedroom. The décor was modern and fresh, with a gray velvet duvet on the kingsize bed, light gray walls, and a wall of mirrored wardrobes. DeeDee took a peek into the bathroom, which was enormous, and had both a walk-in shower and a standalone tub. "Ooh, Al, you're spoiling us!" she said.

When they finished unpacking their clothes, they returned to the open space that was comprised of the living room, dining room, and kitchen, and found Al and Cassie drinking wine.

"Care to join us?" Cassie asked. "We've initiated a nice white."

"That sounds great," DeeDee said. "Just what I need after that flight." She didn't particularly enjoy the hustle bustle of airports and flying.

"How's the investigation going, Al? Do you have any good leads?" Jake asked.

"Not really," Al said. "Jes' got back from seein' Shirley's daughter, Angelina, this afternoon. Her husband Saul's a bad dude, and he chased me down the street. Had to hide in some ol' guy's house, but I did manage to get some face time with her. She tol' me that Surly Sab – a guy in the Mafia I've known fer' a long time – had really outdone hisself cryin' at the funeral. Big red flag. Usually means they're guilty."

"What do you know about this Sab character?" DeeDee asked.

"I know his name is... Sabazio... Lemme' see. Last name is Vinaccia," Al said. "Face got all messed up by one of Shirley's

65

husbands. Dude threw acid all over him. Ain't got no idea why he was at the funeral. Word was he blamed Shirley fer his face 'cuz it was one of her husbands who done it."

"Maybe he was showing his face as a friend so people wouldn't think he was the one who killed her," Cassie said.

"Yeah, that's what Ima thinkin'," Al said. "Anyways… that's a lead I got to follow up on. Angelina didn't say nothin' 'bout anyone else. Said her mom was gettin' death threats up to the day she was offed, but she'd gotten so many Angelina didn't think much 'bout it. Didn't even bother to ask who the threats were from."

"Wow," DeeDee said. "I can't imagine a life like that. Becoming so accustomed to death threats you just shrug them off and carry on."

"Yeah," Al agreed. "That's what I was thinkin', too. Angelina can't have had much of a life with Shirley fer a mother who was killin' husbands left, right, and center." A new thought struck Al. "Wonder who her father is, and if Shirley offed him, too."

Jake leaned forward and put his elbows on his knees. "Does Angelina know her mother was killing her husbands?"

"Didn't ask," Al said. "Ima guessin' when she was younger, she bought all the lies Shirley musta' spun for her. But as she grew up, she musta' realized somethin' weren't quite right."

DeeDee shook her head. "What a childhood. When you met her did she seem okay?"

"Well, she was functionin'," Al said. "Gots herself a newborn son, but after a bit, she opened up and tol' me she wanted to get away from the Mafia life. Problem is, her husband finds it excitin' and don't wanna' leave. Ask me, I'd say he's a major league control freak, and I'll bet my house in the Caymans he's abusin' her.

"When he chased me down the street, he yelled 'bout me talkin' to his woman, and put his hand to his waist, like he was ready to draw out a gun and shoot me. Ima bettin' he's one of them, what do they call it? Oh yeah, a possessive, aggressive type. Doubt he's a little lamb when the bedroom door is closed, if you get my meanin'."

DeeDee shuddered. "Poor girl. I hope she does get away. And without him."

"I suggested that," Al said, "but she didn't look none too happy with me when I said it."

There was a knock on the door, and Al flinched. He hated how he was losing his nerve these days. Back when he'd been in the mob, he'd had a gun, a bulletproof vest, and a fearless attitude to keep him safe. But now? He had something to live for, something to play straight for, and that was Cassie. It made him weak in some ways, stronger in others. Life was different now.

Al put his hand on Red's back and motioned for him to go to the door with him. He figured Red would do whatever he could to protect him. He just hoped it would be enough. He opened the door and Benny strolled into the room like he owned the place.

"Well, hey, hey, hey! If it isn't the lovely Cassie, and Jake and DeeDee, my friends from the Caymans! How are things? How's everybody doing? How do you like this place?"

He kissed Cassie and DeeDee on the cheek, and shook hands with Jake.

"You sound awfully cheerful," Cassie said. "Don't you remember Al is here to investigate a murder and find the killer before they find him?"

"Sure I do," Benny said, throwing his arms up in the air. "Why so serious? You look like you're ready to have another funeral for him. Don't worry yourself for a second. Al is a tough, smart guy. He'll track down the killer, and you'll return to your home on Bainbridge Island, completely out of the game, just a happy couple.

"Consider this as a tourism trip to Chicago, and just enjoy your stay. Al needs all your strength and support, and he's not going to get that with you biting your nails and worrying he's gonna' get shot."

"What've ya' found out?" Al asked.

"Only if you give me the biggest glass of wine in the place," Benny said. "It's worth it 'cuz I've got some great information."

"Spit it out," Al said as he poured the wine.

Benny made himself comfortable in an armchair, or at least tried to, and said, "I hate this modern furniture. They make it look so beautiful and sexy, but when you sit down in one, you feel like you're sitting on a rock. Kind of like a Fred Flintstone sofa. I'd trade this in any day for something a little more worn-in."

"And I'd trade this apartment any day fer a penthouse," Al said pointedly.

"Hmph!" Benny said. "Talk about ungrateful! I tried to get the penthouse, for your information, and it wasn't available. I even offered to pay double the asking price, but they still wouldn't budge."

"I was callin' ya' cheap a li'l while ago," Al said. "Now I got egg all over my face."

Benny grinned as he accepted a glass of wine from Al. "Well, that's one way to describe it. Okay, let's get down to the suspect that I want to tell you about. Do you know Rocco Rosetti?"

"Name sounds sorta' familiar," Al said. "Remind me."

"He's a real loose cannon," Benny said. "Born into the mob, but his father went to jail at a young age. I think his mother was a drug addict and died, but I can't find much information on that. Anyway, he's wild.

"He's pretty dangerous because he's ready to kill just about anyone or anything. He doesn't do what the higher-ups say. Guy just follows his own program. He's committed countless petty robberies, but also some major ones of Mafia drug dealers, too. He has no alliances or allegiances except to himself."

"Wow, he does sound dangerous," DeeDee said.

"Right you are," Benny said. "He is. If he's paid enough, he'll do hits for people from time to time. Rumor is he'd been lurking around Shirley's salon in the weeks running up to her murder."

"Coulda' been he was just involved with her romantically," Al said. "Or maybe he was her next target. Ima thinkin' maybe he found out and got to her first."

Benny grimaced. "That's your imagination running away with you, Al. He's young, far too young for Shirley. And he doesn't have enough money to be the type she'd murder for."

"Okay," Al said. "Then why would he wanna' kill her?"

Benny shrugged. "It might have been a hit. Or maybe she had some information on him. It's a wonder he hasn't been taken out yet, the amount of people he's double-crossed. Trouble is his middle name."

"Great," Al said. "I'll look forward to discussin' Shirley's murder over coffee with him."

Everyone laughed nervously.

"Be very careful, darling," Cassie said. "I know what you're saying, Benny, that we should try to be cheerful. But sometimes I think we should just run away to rural China or somewhere equally remote, and pretend none of this exists."

Al drew her close. "We'll figger it out, Cassie. I promise," he said softly.

She looked at him intensely. "I hope so, Al. I really hope so. I didn't marry you to become a Mafia widow."

CHAPTER TEN

A little while later, DeeDee, Jake, and Cassie had all gone to bed. They'd had a busy day traveling and were tired. The big Indian take-out meal they'd ordered, along with the copious amounts of wine they'd all been drinking, added to their tiredness.

Benny, who had so much stamina he was always the last man standing when it came to talking, and Al, who was too worried to relax, stayed up to talk.

"Benny, I wanna' know more about them other victims," Al said. "Whad'ya know 'bout Butch? What was his name again? That big meal fried my brain."

"Haha! Don't tell me you're losing your touch, Al. His name is Butch Zamora," Benny said. "He was the one who supposedly died of an accidental overdose of his own prescription medication."

"Don't wanna' sound naïve, and I know the Mafia world front to back, but ya' think there's a chance that coulda' happened? Any chance at all?"

"I'd say about the same chance of me turning into a unicorn in front of your eyes, Al," Benny said. "I can smell a mob hit from a mile away. You can too. You're just refusing to smell it because all the roses of your new life are getting in the way."

Al grinned. "Ya' sound jealous."

"A little," Benny said. "Would you feel like a real success if I didn't have a little twinge? It's great to be in love, man. Great to be happy and settled. I'm happy for you."

Benny's own wife had left him once their kids were grown, saying she was looking for romance and adventure, not just making him lasagne and tidying up his socks for the rest of her life. Al conceded she probably did have a point, and guessed that Benny – as much as he loved him – was very hard to live with.

"Thanks," Al said. "Ima deservin' it, right? All that hard work fer the mob year after year. Nearly losin' my life more times than I can count. Deserve some happiness."

Benny leaned forward. "Listen up Al, both the victims were like you. They were in the mob at one time, then got out and tried to live a normal life. It's just too much of a coincidence that it's the same case for all three of you."

Al thought for a moment, and rubbed his forefinger along his upper lip. "Ya' think the only reason for the killin' was that we all left? Ima thinkin' that's pretty extreme."

"I don't know, Al. You know Benny has many theories and many stories, but who knows what the truth is?"

"Didn't really know Butch or the other guy," Al said. "And I never met Shirley. I'd heard of 'em, but they didn't really overlap in our circle, did they?" He paused for a moment to think. "But Shirley certainly had no plans fer leavin' the Mafia."

"But maybe she wanted to," Benny said. "Maybe she'd confided in someone about it. The wrong person. Or someone knew the wrong person and passed the information on."

"Yeah, that's a possibility," Al said. "Don't feel right, though. Call it a hunch. Ima thinkin' there's gotta' be a missin' piece to the puzzle.

Nothin's fittin' together. Only way it would all fit together is if the guy that's been offin' people is a complete psycho."

"What about that Rock guy?" Benny asked. "If there's a psychopath around, he's one. No ties, no obedience, no allegiances. There were rumors he was an informer, or perhaps still is one. Then he went and killed a cop. The guy has no sense of loyalty or code. He just does whatever he wants."

Al shook his head. "Sounds like he thinks he's some kinda immortal."

"I don't know," Benny said. "If you ask me, he's begging to be murdered. But I think no one can get to him. For one thing, he's always moving around. Kind of like a disappearing act. You hear of one killing he's done, then he's nowhere to be found. Maybe he is invincible. I could forgive the guy if that's how he saw himself."

"Ima thinkin' he could definitely be a suspect, though why he'd wanna' kill me I got no clue," Al said. "I mean, if he ain't got no real affiliations, don't see why he'd be mad about me gettin' out of the game."

"Who knows what goes on in that crazy mind of his?"

"What 'bout the other guy who died?"

"Huey Polanski," Benny said. "Fell out of a window when he was sleepwalking." Benny rolled his eyes in mock astonishment. "I mean, come on, not even a five-year-old would believe that one. Apparently the police did, or at least they closed the case. Maybe just because it's a mob hit, or maybe someone paid them off. I'm a bit out of the loop on that one. No idea who's got the cops in their pocket these days, if anyone. I try to stay out of it."

"Very sensible," Al said. "Ima seriously considerin' about what Cassie said. Ya' know, just disappear by goin' somewhere real remote."

"Not a bad idea, if you ask me," Benny said. "I'm not going to lie, I thought you were off your rocker when you said you were coming here to Chicago to play Columbo."

"Ain't playin' Columbo, Benny," Al said, feeling annoyed. "I'm tryin' to keep myself from getting' killed. Track down the killer before they can get to me. Ya' were the one who tipped me off, fer goodness sake."

"I hear that."

"Maybe Cassie's right. I'm worried somethin' might happen to her."

"And rightly so," Benny said. "Clearly, these people don't play around, whoever they are. And they don't hesitate to kill women, either. If I were you, I might just disappear."

Al felt the pressure mounting in his head. "I hear ya', but I can't uproot Cassie from her life. That's the thing. Don't want her to have to drop everythin' 'cuz of my past. I jes' want her to be happy." He felt like his head was going to split in two as he struggled with trying to decide what was the best thing to do.

"Benny, I gotta' see this through to the end. And when I say the end, I don't mean my end. I mean the end, where the killer is locked up behind bars, and Cassie and I ain't gonna' ever hafta' worry again."

Benny raised his wine glass as if toasting Al. "Well, all I can do is wish you the best of luck, and find the best of leads for you."

"Thanks, Benny," Al said. "Yer' a true friend."

"Don't get all soppy on me, Al," Benny said, then flashed him a friendly grin. "You'll be safe, man. You and I know it's dangerous, but I'm sure it'll be fine in the end. It'll work out. It always works out for you."

"Yer' right," Al said. They settled into a comfortable silence. "I wonder if Vinny was alive if he'd be on the hit list."

"Probably," Benny said. "Now, listen to this." He leaned forward and looked Al directly in the eye. "Even though I've said you'll be fine, don't get sloppy. Be careful. Be very, very careful. I don't want another one of my friends to end up on the wrong side of the grass."

CHAPTER ELEVEN

DeeDee and Jake laid in bed, whispering late into the night, neither of them able to sleep.

"I think we can do more to help," Jake said. "We might provide Al with some good cover, because we hardly look like Mafia types. We won't attract too much attention."

DeeDee sighed. "I guess I wanted to leave it to Al and have us just support Cassie. But that's not really good enough, is it? As much as I don't want to face up to it, Al is in very grave danger. He just makes so light of it that I sometimes forget how much danger he's really in."

"We men try to put on a brave face," Jake said. "You know, hold it together for you women. We want you to think that we have everything under control, so you feel safe."

DeeDee stroked him on the arm. "Isn't that lonely, sometimes? Like you have to hold all the worry inside while putting on a brave face?"

"I don't know," Jake said. "Maybe in extreme situations, yeah, or if it goes on a long time."

"Don't you think Al's scared?" DeeDee said. "I would be. And he just sits there cracking jokes and sipping wine like we've come here on a vacation."

"Don't forget, DeeDee, he was in the game for a long time," Jake said. "He's used to dealing with these kinds of situations. This is kind of routine stuff when it comes to the Mafia."

"I suppose," DeeDee said. "It's feels weird to think we're actually caught up in a mob saga. This kind of thing only happens in the movies. Thing is, in the movies, it's all exciting and glamorous. When it happens, it's just freaking scary."

Jake nodded. "The image of the Mafia has definitely been glamorized."

"Kind of like pirates," DeeDee said. "We have all these romantic notions about them now, but really they were just terrible murderous criminals, and the seafaring life consisted of sickness, death, and killing."

"Yes, you're right."

They settled into comfortable silence for a while, leaning up on the pillows, facing each other. "I'm thinking we should offer to interview some of the suspects ourselves," DeeDee said. "That will help Al keep undercover for longer. Plus, it will help keep some of the stress off his shoulders."

Jake nodded. "We'll have to come up with some plausible story for why we're poking around."

"Yes," DeeDee said, "but the problem is, being in the mob, they're going to be very suspicious of outsiders. I would imagine they're used to all kinds of people coming around with bad intentions like undercover cops, hit men, you name it. We'll have to be smart about how we go about this. Very smart."

The sound of a buzzer rang out throughout the apartment. It was very loud, and signified that someone who was downstairs at the reception desk wanted to communicate with someone in the apartment.

Both DeeDee and Jake jumped. DeeDee looked at her watch, then realized she didn't have it on. She grabbed her phone from the bedside table. "It's one in the morning. Who on earth would be buzzing at this time?"

"I don't know," Jake said, "but I've got a very bad feeling about it."

They jumped out of bed and rushed into the living area only to find both Benny and Al sitting dead still, looking at each other with barely-concealed fear on their faces. Cassie was also coming out of her room.

"It's probably just Little Fingers or Joey," Al said, getting up and dusting off his knees. "Nothing to worry about." He walked over towards the intercom.

"Don't," said Benny. "Get in your bedrooms, all of you. I'll handle this." He patted his waistband at the back of his shirt, making it clear he was armed, and started walking towards the main door.

Al continued towards the door, Red with him. "I ain't gonna' hide in fear." He punched the button on the intercom and reception buzzed through.

"Hi, there, we have a package just delivered by a courier for your apartment. Would you like us to bring it up or will you come down?"

Al's mind immediately jumped to the worst. Perhaps it was some kind of bomb or explosive. He didn't want to open it up in the apartment where Cassie and the rest could be hurt. "I'm comin' down," he said. He'd look at it down at the reception desk and decide what to do next.

"Al," Cassie said.

But he left with Red by this side. He didn't turn around or say anything.

Cassie broke down in tears. DeeDee rushed over to her and hugged her.

"I'm gonna' go down there, too," Benny said. "Just in case."

"I'm so worried about him," Cassie sobbed. "Everything makes me tense and edgy. The stress is too much."

"I know, honey," DeeDee said, stroking her hair like she was a little girl. It seemed like Cassie needed to be mothered right then. "This whole situation is just horrible, isn't it?"

Benny managed to thrust his arm into the elevator just before the doors closed. He hopped in beside Al, who kept telling himself to stay calm. It's probably nothin', he thought. Probably nothin' at all.

When they got to the front desk on the ground floor, the receptionist had the package ready and waiting for them. It surprised Al by being a regular-sized envelope, bulked out with some padding. It felt like a small object, such as a bracelet or tiny bottle, had been wrapped in bubble wrap and stuffed into the envelope.

"Thanks," Al said, then turned to Benny. They walked back towards the elevator. "Whad'ya think it is?" he said in a low voice. "Feel it."

He passed the envelope to Benny, who took it in one hand and ran the fingers of his other hand over it. "Couldn't say," he said. "Maybe some kind of jewelry?"

"Yeah, that's what I thought," Al said. "But who would wanna' send me jewelry? Guess if one of the bosses knew I was in town, this could be their way of letting' me know they know I'm here. Maybe I got made at the Russo house." They got into the elevator.

Benny nodded. "Could be a kind of 'welcome back', you know, if they think you're getting back in the game."

"Could be," Al agreed. "There's probably a surveillance camera here in the elevator, and I don't want security knowin' my business, so we'll jes' wait 'til we're back in the apartment to open it. Maybe it'll calm Cassie down. I mean, if it is jewelry, it could be from anyone. Ya' know, someone who likes me or someone who wants me dead. Could be either, but she don't need to know that."

"Yeah, that makes sense," Benny said.

When they walked back into the apartment, they found Cassie, DeeDee, and Jake sitting on the couches in their robes, looking nervous. Al's eyes met Cassie's, and the concern in them pierced straight through to his heart. It even made him a little angry. Why was she doubting his ability to keep himself safe?

Well, he knew very well why, because he was doubting the same thing. That was why it made him mad. She made him face the very feeling he was trying to conceal in himself.

"It's okay!" he announced with a smile. "Jes' a little envelope. We're thinking it's probably jewelry. Maybe someone has spotted me around and wants me to know they know I'm here."

Cassie gasped a little. "Does that mean your cover's been blown?"

"Ain't no a big deal," Al said.

"But…" Cassie began.

Al laughed, though it sounded like it was forced. "Really, it ain't no big deal," he repeated, his voice louder and more intense than he meant it to be. "Let's open this envelope. Maybe I got me a nice new piece of ice."

"Bling bling!" DeeDee said, trying to lighten the mood.

But when Al sat down and opened the envelope, it wasn't a piece of jewelry nestled in the bubble wrap after all.

It was a bullet.

The bubble wrap fell away, and there was a note on a tiny piece of paper coiled around the bullet. Al unwrapped it and read, "Watch your back, the next one has your name on it."

Cassie surprised them all by standing up and throwing her hands in the air. "I can't do this anymore! I didn't sign up for this, Al!"

"Cassie, it'll be fine," he said, trying to sound breezy, though there was a vein throbbing at his temple. "Don't worry, it's just someone tryin' to scare us."

"Well, it's working," Cassie said in a loud voice. "They just delivered this to the apartment building. We need to get out of here, and fast."

"She's right," Benny said. "You'll have to relocate. It's too risky, even with the windows being bulletproof."

Al thought quickly. "Okay, well it's clear my cover's been blown and the people who wanna' kill me know I'm here. So now it don't make no sense to try and hide. In fact, Ima thinkin' we need to get as visible as possible. Make everyone turn heads when they see us. More public we are, the better. That way it's gonna' be hard for anyone to make a move without bein' spotted."

He looked at Benny, then at DeeDee and Jake, and then at Cassie. "Ha," he said, laughing. "I got the best idea. What's the most expensive hotel in Chicago? Maybe the Four Seasons?"

"Likely," Benny said. "I prefer the Langham, though. Good staff. Wonderful bathrooms. Food's great, too."

"All right," Al said. "We'll be goin' there and bookin' the best suite in the place."

They left within minutes and finally managed to get some restful sleep once they'd registered at the Langham Hotel and been shown to the penthouse suite.

The next morning, they all slept in until 10:30 a.m., and had missed the hotel breakfast. Of course, it was the Langham and they were staying in the penthouse, so they could order whatever they wanted, whenever they wanted it.

They ended up having a long, lazy breakfast of pastries and toast and muffins, along with coffee and tea. Al surprised them by being in a very good mood, as if he'd anonymously been sent a bundle of cash the night before, rather than a bullet.

"Now," he said, wiping his hands down on a napkin and grinning. "We're gonna' have us some fun."

The rest of that day was filled with the most surreal experiences any of them had ever had, and it was so much fun they almost managed to forget there was any murder threat at all.

When they got into a cab, Al briefed them on his idea. "Okay, guys, so we gotta' get as visible as possible now, right? Here's what we're gonna' do. We hit Saks Fifth Avenue, and go and buy the most luxurious, wildest, brightest, boldest clothes we can. Seriously, don't matter if'n we look ridiculous! All we've gotta' do is turn heads wherever we go."

Benny grinned. "Al, I love it when you're in town. I'm chipping into this, folks. Money is no object!" Benny loved to dress flamboyantly, and with direct instruction to do so, he was about to have a field day!

"Then we're gonna' hit one of the best restaurants tonight, and a play. Maybe even go to an art gallery. Need to be showin' our faces everywhere. I want everyone to know Al's in town. That way all my supporters can come out of the woodwork."

Jake shook his head, laughing with bewilderment. "Well, I

certainly hadn't predicted this is what I'd be doing this week."

"Me neither," Al said. "And I know it's a crazy plan, but we gotta' have us some fun, right? Okay by ya', Cassie?"

"Yes, I think so," she said. "This feels a little better, getting ourselves out in the open. But don't you think we should tell the police about the bullet you were sent?"

"Unfortunately, the police won't be interested," Benny said. "They might even arrest Al for having an unlicensed bullet in his possession. More likely they'd just do nothing at all. When it comes to the mob, they don't want to know. They let us carry out our own justice, behind the scenes."

Cassie bit her lip. "Yes, I know. That's what worries me."

CHAPTER TWELVE

Once they were in Saks Fifth Avenue, everyone cheered up. How could they not? Their mission was to find the craziest, most eye-catching clothes they could and then buy them. And they had a great time doing it.

DeeDee and Cassie had quite a time in the hats section, trying on the most bizarre hats in all kinds of weird and wonderful shapes and colors.

"Perhaps this is a little too eye-catching," Cassie said, taking off a fluorescent yellow hat with feathers sticking out of it.

"You think?" DeeDee asked with a chuckle.

As they wandered through the store, Cassie began to loosen up. The frown lines on her forehead disappeared, and she started to smile a bit more often. By the time they were in the women's clothing section, she was positively giddy.

They loaded up with all kinds of garish outfits — bright African print trouser suits, dazzling sequined dresses, and wide-leg jumpsuits in polka dots. The woman manning the dressing room raised an eyebrow when she checked in their selections.

Then it was time for the fashion show!

"Oh my goodness," DeeDee called out to Cassie in the next cubicle with a laugh, as she slipped into a hot pink minidress. "I'm not sure I can get away with this." She came out of the cubicle and posed in front of the mirror, laughing at herself. "Definitely can't."

Then Cassie opened the door to her dressing room wearing towering gold high heels and a glittering gold bodysuit to match. Her shoulders were hunched in on herself, like she was trying to hide her body.

"Oh, Cassie, you look fantastic," DeeDee said. "Just like a movie star!"

Cassie looked herself up and down in the mirror. "I do not," she said. "I look like someone's mother trying to join their daughter at a nightclub. I look downright embarrassing."

DeeDee grinned. "I'll grant you that the outfit is a little young, but that still doesn't stop you from looking fantastic. I think you should buy it. You'll certainly cheer Al up."

"Unfortunately, you're probably right. I bet he'd love it," Cassie said with an eye roll.

"I'm sure half the men in Chicago will love it, too," DeeDee said, laughing.

"But look at you! You look absolutely gorgeous."

"Negative," DeeDee said with a grin. "With this dress, I'm just a slash of red lipstick and some high boots away from looking like a streetwalker."

Just then, a very elegant looking older woman came in with some mature and ladylike clothing draped over her arm. She widened her eyes in shock at the pair of them standing there in their skimpy clothes, then gave them a disapproving frown as she went into her own cubicle.

"Well, I guess she told us," Cassie whispered.

"Yup. Isn't it fun?" DeeDee whispered back, trying not to laugh. She knew they were being childish, but it felt wonderful to be silly and carefree, even if was just for a little while. Anything to stop thinking about how much danger Al was in.

"Let's try on some other things," said Cassie. "Some longer things."

The next round was entirely different. Cassie came out of her room wearing a red sequinned strapless dress that skimmed the floor, while DeeDee wore a floating dress in peacock colors – blue, purple, green, and a touch of muted light grass green – that she'd have never normally picked out, but which made her look gorgeously elegant.

"Now that's a lot better," Cassie said. "We both look much better."

"I agree," DeeDee said. She turned around in front of the mirror to look at herself from all angles, and the dress floated out a little in the most pleasing way. "I wasn't at all sure about this when it was on the rack."

"It looks fantastic on you," Cassie said. "The colors really make your eyes pop."

DeeDee and Cassie walked out of the dressing room wearing their new dazzling dresses. The dressing room assistant snipped off the tags for them, and the cashier rang them up. Then they shopped for accessories. The flats Cassie was wearing didn't match the dress at all and DeeDee's sneakers looked ridiculous with her glamorous new attire.

They went to the shoe section so they could get something more suitable to match their purchases. DeeDee picked out some patent high heeled sandals in navy, while Cassie went for golden wedge sandals. They finished their outfits off with a sparkly gold clutch for Cassie and a navy blue one for DeeDee.

"Let's find Jake and Al," said DeeDee. "We can show off our new looks."

"I think we should call them," Cassie said. "If we traipse around the store looking for them, I'll only get nervous."

"Good idea. Besides, we're not exactly wearing comfortable traipsing shoes, are we?"

"Definitely not." Cassie got out her cell phone and called Al.

He didn't pick up. DeeDee watched as Cassie's confident face creased into worry again. She didn't look at DeeDee, just tapped on the phone to hang up, then tapped again to make the call for the second time. Then she started pacing. By the time she made the third call, she was beginning to look around the store every which way, panic written all over her face.

"I'm sure everything's fine," DeeDee said, though she was beginning to feel a little nervous in spite of herself. It seemed the worry was catching.

"Call Jake," Cassie said.

DeeDee's voice was soothing. "Seriously, Cassie, I wouldn't worry." She took her phone out of her new navy clutch and called Jake. There was no answer.

It was as if someone had flicked a switch in Cassie. She threw her arms up in the air. "Someone's got them, I just know it. I knew it was a terrible idea to come to Chicago. Now he's been spotted, and I'll bet you money that both of them have been kidnapped. Maybe they'll let Jake go, but they sure won't let Al go anywhere. I think it's because he knows too much, that's why they want to kill him." She began to choke back tears with a thick voice.

"Why aren't they answering their phones?" She called again and continued her fearful stream of consciousness. "I love that man so much, and I hate myself for loving him and thinking that all the mob stuff wouldn't matter. I thought it was romantic, you know? A reformed man who wanted to live the rest of his life in peace.

"I felt sorry for him. He got pulled into it when he was little more than a child. And now he regrets everything that went on and wants to live a good life, but someone doesn't want that to happen. I'm sure they're watching us and tracking down our every move. The bullet! They probably followed us from the hotel all the way down here, and now they've got Al, and…"

Just then someone tapped her on her shoulder causing Cassie to pretty much jump out of her skin. There was Al, grinning from ear to ear, dressed in an emerald green tuxedo. "We clash horribly, huh, babe? Red and green. We look like a Christmas decoration."

Cassie was so relieved she burst into a half-laugh, half-cry. She punched him on the arm. "You! I was worrying myself crazy."

DeeDee agreed, "She was even getting me concerned. I'm glad you're both all right." She looked Jake up and down. He was wearing a black shirt emblazoned with huge red roses, tight black jeans, and shiny black leather shoes. "Wow. Well, you look… interesting."

"Interesting?" Jake asked, looking back at Al. "Dashing, handsome, incredibly sexy… those were the words I thought would come to mind."

It was so strange to see Jake wearing clothes like that. DeeDee looked at him and nodded. He did look good, after all. "I think I could learn to like it. Watch out, or I might want you to make that your new style!"

"I used to dress like that in my younger days," Al said. "Now, come." He led all of them over to a mirror, and gestured at the reflection in the mirror. "Don't we look like a glamorous crew?"

"Indeed we do!" Cassie said.

They noticed that as people were passing them by, they turned their heads to look again and almost stare in disbelief.

"Looks like we're attracting some attention," Jake said.

"That's exactly what we want," Al said. "Right, come on. Let's go and experience the best Chicago has to offer."

They strutted out of the department store like superstars, and hailed a cab outside. "To the Mango Tree," Al said to the driver, as they all slipped into the back. He called Benny and invited him to join them.

Soon they were all sitting in the exclusive Thai restaurant at a table by the window – at Al's request, to make them more visible. Rather than ordering individual dishes, they went for the Royal Feast for five. Along with plenty of beer and wine, their table was quickly graced with Pad Thai, chicken curry, Tom Yum prawn soup, pork and peanut curry, beef stir-fry, steamed fish, rice noodles, fried rice, and a number of other dishes.

"Wowza," Benny said. "You're really spoiling us, Al. I hope you don't think I'm paying for any of this, by the way."

Al tutted and shook his head. "Despite you sounding cheaper than a bag of potato chips, you'd be right about that, buddy. We've left that apartment open, uh? What will you do with it?"

Benny shrugged, not seeming to be bothered by what Al said. He started to load up his plate from the dishes in the center of the table. "I'll probably AirBnb it. I don't know. As long as you don't have a bullet hole in your head, I don't really care." That brought down the tone a little, but Benny didn't seem to notice. Cassie was already biting her nails again, and the table became silent except for the sounds of cutlery clinking against the plates.

Al sighed. "I was gonna' save the gory talk fer later, but since ya' brought it up, got any more leads? This is gettin' serious now. I'm gonna' get proactive and visit as many people as I can. Don't make sense to hide my face anymore."

"Finally," Benny said. "I've been waiting to hear that since you got here. Well, you already know about that crazy Rock guy, Rocco Rosetti. Dunno' if I'd wanna' visit him personally, though. He might blow your head off for just looking at him the wrong way. Next thing you know, your body's chopped up into tiny pieces and found in a garbage can somewhere."

"That's a comforting thought," DeeDee said, suppressing a shiver and avoiding looking over at Cassie.

"Just real life, sweetheart," said Benny. "When you're in the mob, you hear this kind of thing every day of your life."

"Please don't go and see him," Cassie said to Al.

He put his large hand on hers in a comforting way, and gave her a deep, regretful look, but he couldn't make any promises. "Who else?" he asked Benny.

"I'd go see Betty Traxel," Benny said. "The Cook. She runs the Bella Rosa restaurant, pretty upscale place."

"Yeah, I remember her," Al said.

"She lets people use her back room for all sorts of shady activities, but she has no real alliances except for…" He rubbed his fingers together, indicating cash. "If you take enough up there and she knows anything, you'll get to know it pretty fast, too."

Al frowned. "From what I heard, she don't like strangers."

Benny nodded, his mouth stuffed full of Pad Thai. "There is that," he said thickly. "Maybe the women could go instead. Soften her up a little."

"I'm certainly willing," DeeDee said. "Anything to see this killer caught."

Cassie nodded, but she was obviously still nervous. Her darting eyes betrayed the fact she wanted to be on an exotic island sipping a cocktail and reading a trashy novel, not in the middle of a Chicago Mafia ring trying to catch a dangerous murderer before he caught Al. DeeDee saw her look, and made up her mind to be strong for Cassie. After all, she couldn't begin to imagine how scary it must be to have your husband wanted by Mafia hitmen.

"Why would she want to kill Al?" DeeDee asked. "And Shirley?"

Benny's eyes brightened. He loved to tell a story. "Well, she was once in love with a guy called Tommaso. Then Shirley turned his head, married him, and later killed him. Even though it happened years ago, some people hold grudges for a long time. Revenge is a dish best served cold, as they say."

"Hmm," Al said, "but whatta' 'bout me?"

"You never know with her," Benny said. "Like I said, she's motivated by money. There could be any number of reasons. Or maybe someone paid her to organize the hit on you. Who knows?"

"Who else?" Al asked Benny.

"Porky's due in town."

"Porky?" Al asked. "I thought he got outta' the game ages ago."

"Yeah, he did," said Benny. "Doing crazy real estate in Florida. But he still has a gym here. Comes back from time to time to check over things, and flirt with the female fitness trainers. Despite that big belly of his, he could beat pretty much anyone in a weightlifting contest. Some of the girls go wild over that. And his money, of course."

"He was married to Shirley at one time," Al explained to the others. "He's the only husband that got out of the marriage alive. Maybe he still holds a grudge from when she tried to kill him, and so he sent someone to put her lights out. Being in Florida is a great cover."

"Sure is," said Benny. "Go check out Surly Sab as well. He's the one that got his face disfigured by..."

"One of Shirley's husbands," Al finished. "I know. Shirley's daughter said he made a big cryin' scene at the funeral, too, so he's definitely on my radar. So we got The Rock, The Cook, Porky, and Surly Sab. Anybody else?"

"This one's a long shot," Benny said, "but Little Fingers mentioned Hank Mitchell's wife. Remember Hank?"

Al paused. "Don't ring a bell."

"I'm not surprised. Boring as sin, that guy is. He does some accounting for the Ferrari family..."

"The Ferrari family?" Jake asked.

"He wishes," Benny said with a snort. "Ferrari is a pretty common surname in Italian circles. And whispers are he's been involved in a couple of hits. He makes a great cover because he's so, so numbingly boring and regular, no one looks at him twice."

"Quite the opposite of you then," DeeDee joked.

"Quite the opposite of all of you," Benny countered, gesturing at their clothes. "I was too hungry to notice, but now I see you all look like something out of a rap video."

Al laughed. "I gotta' get myself a huge gold chain to complete the look. We're jes' bein' visible, Benny, that's all. Now, you said it's Hank Mitchell's wife I should go see. Why's that? Why'd she wanna' kill Shirley?"

"Search me," said Benny. "She was overheard at the Langham, where you're staying, making some bad comments about Shirley, Little Fingers told me. That ain't much to go on, but something tells me she might be worth checking up on."

Al nodded. "More the better. So we got's five people we gotta' check out." He smiled and said, "Sounds like a plan."☐

CHAPTER THIRTEEN

That evening, Al gave DeeDee and Cassie the task of going to Betty Traxel's restaurant and getting whatever information they could. They wore their brand new clothes, fixed up their hair and makeup, and ended up looking like two exceptionally rich women going out to dinner to discuss their plans for taking over the world.

"Be careful," Jake whispered to DeeDee, squeezing her hand. He gave her a kiss on the cheek.

"I will," she said, her head held high. She felt more invigorated than afraid, and was determined to be strong for Cassie.

"Jes' whatever you do, don't go into her office," Al said. "That woman sells plenty of cocaine. Might be some rough characters in there, along with her."

In the cab on the way to the restaurant, Cassie was surprisingly cheerful. "I finally feel like I'm doing something to help," she said. "All that waiting around and worrying about Al was getting to me. I'm so glad he and Jake are having a guy's night in, and I'm the one out."

"Now he can worry about you," DeeDee chuckled. "But we'll be totally fine."

"Yes, we will," Cassie said. "I spoke to Benny about this Betty Traxel woman, and he said she's not particularly loyal to anybody. She stays to herself, and wants to avoid as much drama as possible. It doesn't look like she's going to turn around and shoot us."

"I certainly hope not!" DeeDee laughed. "Welcome to Chicago. Bang, you're dead."

It was surreal to be laughing and joking about something so serious, but they needed the light relief.

"I don't know if I'll be able to eat much, though," Cassie said. "I had so much at lunch."

"Me too," DeeDee said. "I still feel full. We can just nibble, and look like ladies who only eat salads."

Cassie grinned. "That might be a good thing."

When they arrived at the Bella Rosa restaurant the cab stopped directly in front of it. A doorman came over to the cab and opened their doors. Deedee looked over at Cassie and wiggled her eyebrows. "Fancy," she whispered. She half expected the doorman to take her hand and pull her out of the cab, like she was some sort of a queen, but he didn't.

"Welcome, ladies," he said. "This way." He opened the door and ushered them into the restaurant.

It was quite dark inside, which was a little intimidating. Every surface was black and shiny, and the lights were dimmed low. It looked very luxurious indeed. They were welcomed by a man in a tuxedo.

"Good evening, and welcome to Bella Rosa," he said. "Table for two?"

"Please," Cassie said. Her voice sounded quite posh, like she was putting an accent on, and DeeDee made a mental note to tease her about it later.

He led them to a table right in the middle of the restaurant, took their coats, and held chairs out for them. "I'll bring you the wine list and our menus," he said. "I hope you'll enjoy your dinner with us."

As soon as he was gone, DeeDee said, "That was quite a posh accent you put on just then."

Cassie laughed and pushed her head into her hands. "Oh, gosh, really? Al says that sometimes, you know, that when we go to fancy places, my voice changes. How embarrassing."

"Well, his voice never changes wherever he goes," said DeeDee. "Booming and confident as ever."

"That's just it," said Cassie. "He's so confident. Wherever he goes, it's like he owns the place. You know, it's happened more than once when we've been in some high-end place. I think once we were in an art gallery, and once we were in an antique store. Customers came up to him thinking he was the owner!"

"No way!" DeeDee said with a laugh. "That's so funny. I guess he has a real presence about him."

Cassie nodded. "Wish I did. I feel like a little fish out of water in these kinds of places. I think I put on the accent without realizing it, trying to fit in, I guess."

"That's very insightful," DeeDee said. "Well, I say as long as you can pay the bill, you belong."

"Good point!"

"Although I am surprised that you still feel that way after all the high-end restaurants you've reviewed for your column in the Seattle Times."

"You'd think so, but obviously I still do," Cassie said.

The waiter brought the wine list and the menus as promised, and the women looked them over.

DeeDee looked up at Cassie, her mouth in a round O. "See the prices on this menu?" she whispered. "This Betty Traxel must be a multimillionaire if the amount she's charging is any indication."

"I know!" Cassie said. "One of these main courses, look, the one with the lobster. It's $175.00."

DeeDee chuckled. "We're living large, Cassie."

"I'll say."

They both ordered white wine and chicken salad. DeeDee had considered the prawn option instead, but she'd had so many at lunch she felt like having something different.

When they were halfway through their meal, Cassie whispered, "Ooh, look! A large woman with a black velvet trouser suit and tons of gold jewelry came out of a side office and went up to the bar. "Do you think that's her?"

"Could be," DeeDee said. "Benny said she looked formidable, and that woman certainly does."

"Doesn't she just?" Cassie said. "I doubt even the toughest Mafia men would dare mess with her."

They watched her as the bartender poured her a large shot of vodka, a double, or perhaps even a triple, in a crystal glass. She knocked it back in one gulp.

DeeDee raised her eyebrows at Cassie with a smile. "She looks like she can hold her booze, too."

Then the bartender poured her a glass full of creamy liqueur, which she picked up and took back to her office. Just before she went through the door, she turned and looked back at the room. Her eyes rested on Cassie, who had been looking at her, and Cassie quickly looked away.

"Oh gosh," Cassie whispered.

The woman turned back and went into the office, closing the door behind her.

"What?" DeeDee asked.

"She looked at me, and it was like a bolt of lightning went through my body. That woman's dangerous, I can just tell."

DeeDee felt a little nervous. "Let's go talk to her. Right now. Before we chicken out."

Cassie gestured at their half-eaten meals. "But…"

"Don't worry, they'll wait for us," DeeDee said. "Come on."

Before Cassie could argue any further, DeeDee stood up and walked towards the office door. Cassie hurried after her, then hovered by the door, looking worried.

"We can do this," DeeDee said firmly, then knocked on the door three times and stuck her chin in the air. She turned to see Cassie looking straight forward, with much more confidence. That made her smile.

"What?" a voice called out from inside.

DeeDee took a deep breath and tried the door, but it was locked.

A moment later the door opened. The woman standing here had her hand on the back of her waistband, as if she had a gun and was ready to blast away if necessary.

"Oh, hello," she said, fixing her face into a fake smile. "How can I help you?" There was something very hostile about her tone, even though it was sickly sweet.

"Hi there," Cassie said. "I'm Al De Cuco's wife." That was what Al had told her to say. He and Betty knew each other, though somewhat distantly.

"And I'm friends with both of them," DeeDee added.

"I see." She gave them a genuine smile. "Come in, please, come in. I'm Betty Traxel."

They hesitated, remembering Al's warning.

"Um…." DeeDee looked at Cassie, the unspoken question about whether they should go in spoken clearly in their eyes.

Betty roared with laughter. "What's the problem? You think I'm gonna' kill ya'?"

"Of course not," Cassie quickly said. "Okay, we'll come in."

DeeDee wished she'd brought some kind of weapon with her. Even the knife from their dinner table would have been better than nothing. She mentally ran through the contents of her navy clutch, but lipstick, tissues, and a compact mirror weren't suitable weapons, unless she was thinking of giving Betty a makeover.

Betty sat behind the desk. "I heard Al was in town."

DeeDee and Cassie looked at each other.

"That was quick," Cassie said. "He only arrived a couple of days ago."

"Chicago news spreads like wildfire," Betty said. "Heard he had quite a spectacular funeral, too." She laughed a deep belly laugh.

"Yes," Cassie said, blushing a little from embarrassment. "I suppose you also know he's been getting death threats?"

"No, I didn't," Betty said. "I assumed he faked his death to start a new life somewhere else, Europe perhaps, free from the watchful eyes of the mob."

"That would have been a good plan," Cassie said. "Anyway, he's here in town trying to find out who murdered Shirley Morris, since it may well be the same person that wants to kill him."

"I don't know much about that," Betty said briskly. "I make a point of not involving myself in people's business."

DeeDee frowned. "But you just said…"

"I said news in Chicago travels fast. I didn't say I was privy to people's assassination plans. That's none of my business. And I make sure it stays none of my business. Do you understand?"

"So you're telling us you don't know anything at all about who killed Shirley?"

"No, and even if I did, I wouldn't tell you."

"Do you know something?" DeeDee probed.

"What are you, a couple of skinny Inspector Poirots?" Betty asked. She leaned back in her chair with a cocky smile and sipped on her liqueur. "I hope you know you're playing with fire. Dicing with death. Al's a great guy, but he's a fool sending you here doing this. Get him to get you on a flight to the Seychelles or something with a connecting flight to somewhere else, in case there's any mob at the airport. This might look like fun and games at the movies, but in reality it's more like life and death."

Cassie and DeeDee decided to walk back to the hotel, since it was only a few blocks away through a safe, upscale area that was bustling with nightlife. The wind was quite cold, but it was refreshing after the heat and darkness of the restaurant.

"Well, she told us," DeeDee said. "Maybe you were right to be so worried."

Cassie held her head high and said, "I don't know why, but what she said lit a fire in me. Like she thought we were small-town losers who couldn't handle anything. I've made up my mind to be totally confident now. As confident as Al and Benny. Everything's going to be absolutely fine. I have faith that we can bring the killer to justice and live a happy life, free from mob threats. I just know it."

"That's the spirit!" DeeDee said, inspired by Cassie's speech. "I can't wait to get home and get these high heels off. We can chill for the night with the guys and really relax. Then it's full speed investigation tomorrow."

"I need to call Briana and Liam and tell them what's going on," Cassie said. "All I told them was that I was going to leave Bainbridge for a while. They're probably getting a little worried about me."

"Like telling them what's really going on isn't going to worry them," DeeDee said.

"I'm sure it will, but I'll feel better doing it," Cassie said as they entered the hotel.

CHAPTER FOURTEEN

But that evening was not as relaxing as DeeDee and Cassie had hoped it would be.

When they got back to their suite at the Langham, they found Little Fingers, Joey, and Benny there, as well as Al and Jake, so there was certainly no chance of a cozy night in. There were empty pizza boxes and beer cans strewn across the dining room table, and a lively game of cards was in progress. It was so lively, in fact, that it barely registered on anyone that DeeDee and Cassie had returned.

"Hey, babe!" Al said, only momentarily turning away from the card game. "Naw, Little Fingers, ya' gotta' be kiddin' me. Think yer' foolin' me with that bluff?"

Cassie seemed just as unimpressed as DeeDee felt when they looked at each other. But then her face softened. "Let's leave them alone for a while," she said. "Any kind of respite from the tension Al's under is welcome."

DeeDee nodded. "I think you're right. Anyway, I need to change out of these heels and this dress. Cozy slippers, here I come!"

"I'm with you," Cassie said.

"See you in a while."

DeeDee decided to make the most of everyone being busy, and take a long soak in the luxurious bathtub in their private bathroom. It was huge, and marble tiling graced every surface. The enormous corner bath had jacuzzi jets inside it and was big enough for two or even three people, more like a hot tub. She ran hot water in it, and poured in plenty of the complementary bubble bath, Moroccan Incense & Honey flavor, which made the whole bathroom smell glorious.

Her hands and feet were still a little cold from their walk, and stung somewhat as she slid into the hot foamy water.

"This is the life," she said out loud, and it echoed around the bathroom. She'd turned the lights down low on the dimmer switch, and it was so incredibly relaxing she hoped she wouldn't fall asleep.

As she lay back, luxuriating in the bubbles, she thought about their encounter with Betty. DeeDee thought it was likely Betty knew more than she let on. She was a strange character. It was interesting that she was deeply intertwined with the Mafia and knew everything that went on, yet she'd said she didn't want to get involved in other people's business. That just didn't make sense, did it?

She thought more about Tommaso, and wished she'd had the courage to bring his name up when they'd talked to Betty. She was such a formidable character, and DeeDee was sure she'd touched the back of her waist to reach for a gun, so DeeDee hadn't felt comfortable mentioning his name.

It was clearly a very personal subject for Betty, and DeeDee hadn't wanted to venture into emotional territory. She'd seen enough movies to know that when gangsters and their ilk felt uncomfortable, they'd often rather shoot than cry. Still, she kind of regretted it. They really hadn't found out much at all from their visit with Betty.

DeeDee didn't realize how much time she'd whiled away in the bathtub, thinking, until she heard a knock on the door. "Hi, love," Jake said. "Can I come in?"

"Of course," DeeDee said.

"I won the poker game," Jake said, his eyes shining with excitement.

"That's great," DeeDee said and smiled up at him. "And against Benny, too. How much did you win?"

"Oh, just $5," he said. "We played with dimes. Al and Benny told me a long story about how they used to play poker all the time with their friends, for real money, you know, thousands and thousands. But then one night it got sour, and somebody got shot. They didn't die, but after that they've never played for an amount big enough that anyone might get emotional about."

"Whoa," DeeDee said. "These guys are full of stories, huh?"

Jake's eyes widened. "You don't know the half of it. With all that beer, Al's tongue got a little loose, and they were regaling me with tales of their 'prime' days in the Mafia, when they were in their early 20s. It was some serious stuff. Anyway, how did it go at the restaurant?"

"Honestly, it was a bust," DeeDee said. "I'm pretty sure Betty had a gun in her waistband and she was very... well, intimidating. We didn't get any information out of her. She said she really didn't know anything about Shirley, which I'm not sure I believe. I mean, she already knew Al was in town. How could she not know about one of the most significant murders in the mob in years? That just doesn't add up."

"Hmm," said Jake. "Maybe she thought you guys were undercover cops or something."

"Nah," DeeDee said. "She knew Cassie was Al's wife. She knew all about the fake funeral, too."

"I have to agree with you. She does seem to be in the know."

"Yes. There's something about Shirley's murder she doesn't want us to know."

"Maybe because she did it," Jake said. "That would be an easy explanation, wouldn't it?"

"If only it were that simple, and we could all get out of here and go back to our normal lives. No more sniffing around the mob." She paused. "You know, sometimes I have to pinch myself. Can you believe what we're doing?"

Jake grinned down at her. "Think of it as the spice of life."

"Easy for you to say," she said, chuckling. "Our lives are in danger, aren't they? I can't work it out. One minute I feel fine and totally confident, like we're going to solve this case any moment now. Then the next minute I'm totally paranoid and watching over my shoulder all the time. I think Cassie's going through the same thing."

Jake nodded. "I'd say Al is, too."

"And what about you?"

"Hmm… I'm fine. As a private investigator, you get used to all this life and death stuff. It's exciting. We're living in a movie, babe."

DeeDee playfully splashed him with water from the bath. "This is not a movie!"

It was a fun argument. Sometimes DeeDee and Jake loved to banter back and forth like that when the occasion was right.

But then they heard yelling in the other room, and then someone else shouting. It definitely did not sound like a fun argument. Jake's eyes went wide.

"What's going on?" DeeDee asked.

"Let me go check," Jake said, frowning.

"I'm coming, too." DeeDee scrambled out of the bath, foam still clinging to her body, threw on a robe, and ran out behind Jake as they rushed through the bedroom and into the main room where the voices were coming from.

It was Cassie and Al, shouting at each other. DeeDee was shocked. She'd never even seen them raise their voice towards one another.

"What's going on?" Jake said in a loud voice to them.

DeeDee noticed Little Fingers and Benny slipping out of the door of the hotel suite, trying not to be noticed.

Cassie was wild-eyed and clearly furious. "Al thinks it's a wonderful idea to arm himself with a bulletproof vest and a gun!" She gestured at the items he was clutching, her arm shaking.

"I got to," Al said passionately. "Ima thinkin' this is startin' to get more dangerous. Whad'ya want me to do, turn up at the murderer's house completely vulnerable like I got a bull's eye painted on my back? Fer me to get myself killed?"

"No, of course not!" Cassie yelled. "But neither do I want a Mafia man for a husband, who walks around wearing a bulletproof vest. This isn't some gangster movie, Al. This is your life, my life, our lives. Haven't you left all of this behind? Weren't we going to go to the police?"

DeeDee didn't know what to say. She could see both points of view, Cassie was being dragged into a Mafia life she'd never wanted and knew nothing about, while Al was trying to protect his life, find the killer, and move on. It felt like one great big mess.

"I'm sorry," Al said in a loud voice. "What else do ya' want me to do? I'm tryin' to put this to bed, Cassie! I'm trying to do this so as we can move on with our life. Whad'ya think I am, some kinda' wizard? That I can jes' go back in time and change my past? Whad'ya want from me?"

"Nothing!" Cassie yelled. "Nothing at all!" She took her wedding ring off and placed it on the kitchen counter. Then she turned to Al with pure resentment in her eyes. "Nothing at all," she repeated, but this time very quietly, and it was like a knife cutting through the air. Then she went into their bedroom and slammed the door.

"Ugh!" Al raged. "There is no pleasin' that woman!" He sank down on the couch, his head in his hands. It looked like he was about to cry tears of pure frustration. Red walked over to Al and put his head in his lap, sensing something was wrong.

Jake sat beside him, while DeeDee went to see Cassie. She opened the door slowly, and found Cassie curled up against the headboard of the luxurious bed, crying her eyes out.

"Sorry," Cassie said, trying to hold the sobs back.

"It's okay," DeeDee said. "Cry if you need to." She drew her close in a hug which made Cassie start crying in full force again.

"You must think I'm horrible," Cassie said, drawing away from the hug and leaning back. She wiped her eyes, her fingers blackening from her mascara. "I just didn't sign up for any of this."

"I know," DeeDee said softly.

"When Al and I got together, he assured me he was done with all of that life. That he'd never again carry a gun. That we'd just live a regular existence like other folks. No drama. No Mafia. Then this happens. And I know it's not his fault. Which makes me feel so guilty."

Her face crumpled. "I know he didn't want this to happen, didn't expect it. But that doesn't change the fact that it is happening, and it's connected with his past. I don't want to be horrible about it, but I just feel so worried about him all the time, and worried about me, and about you and Jake, too. This is a mess, and it just shouldn't be happening."

DeeDee nodded. "That sounds like a lot of mixed feelings."

"Yes. I suppose it does, but I do have mixed feeling, just like you said." She let out a little sob. "I shouldn't have left my ring out there. I don't mean I want to break up with Al. I love him so much, more than I ever thought it was possible to love someone. But this is all just too much right now. And I can't help blaming him, even if it is a little unfair. Is it unfair? I don't even know anymore."

"I certainly don't have the answers," DeeDee said. "I think he's a good man, and he's trying to deal with this situation in the best way he can for both of you. That doesn't mean you're not entitled to your feelings, though. I can see why you're angry and confused and have just had enough. It's a pretty big load for one person to bear."

"Yes," Cassie said. Then she looked down at her hands. "But it's not just me, is it? It's him, you, Jake and me. We can all do this together."

DeeDee smiled. "You bet. In fact, we are doing this together. Our meeting with Betty didn't get us that far, but it was a good start. We were very brave, the two of us."

Cassie chuckled. "We were, weren't we?"

"Absolutely!" DeeDee said. "And I'm sure Al won't need the vest or the gun, really. It's just to make him feel safer."

Cassie frowned. "I'm fine with the vest, just not the gun… Maybe Benny could go with him and carry the gun instead?"

"Good idea," said DeeDee. "I'll bet Al would welcome that suggestion."

CHAPTER FIFTEEN

Al was actually relieved at the suggestion Cassie made to have Benny carry the gun for him. He'd carried a gun occasionally since his days in the mob, but it still made him feel uncomfortable. At some point he'd even vowed never to carry one again. But that was before this situation had developed.

The next morning, he put his bulletproof vest on underneath his clothes, and felt glad for the protection. He was probably being overly paranoid. He hoped he was, but anything to make him and Cassie feel safer was more than welcome.

Cassie and DeeDee decided to head down to the spa for the morning. They were also planning on going to a charity event that Hope was hosting that evening. They left the penthouse talking about massage treatments and wraps and facials. Jake wanted to see more of Chicago, so he took off with his phone set to Maps.

Benny and Al took a taxi to Porky's gym. It was well known in the mob that in addition to his real estate projects in Florida, he had a chain of gyms, with the largest being in Chicago. Benny had also let Al know that Porky had come to town to check up on it. He didn't trust people to do things properly for him, because of the number of times he'd been burned in the past.

Al decided not to go in with the mob angle and instead play it cool. He and Benny walked into the shining, modern gym, and went over to the sleek reception desk. "Hi there," he said. "I wanna' join."

"Great," the beautiful hard-body receptionist said with a huge smile. She took out a clipboard with a form on it and slid it across the desk.

"Thanks," Al said. "I got a few questions before I join. I wanna' talk to the manager."

The receptionist looked up at him. "Anything I can help you with?"

Al thought quickly. "It's kinda' sensitive information. The manager is best."

The receptionist paused for a moment, looking at him a little warily. "Okay," she said. She pressed a button on her phone, and said, "I have two gentlemen who want to see you." She gestured towards the waiting area, and Benny and Al sat down.

Before long the manager came in the room and stepped over to where they were sitting. He was a very pale man with a tall skinny stature, wearing a tracksuit. "I'm Killian Mathers," he said. "Manager of Porky's Gym. How can I help?"

"Hi there," Al said, getting up and giving him a handshake. "Nice meetin' ya'. Is Donald Richards still the owner of this place?"

"Yes." Killian gave them a wary look which made Al certain he was well informed about Porky's Mafia connections. "Do you want to speak to him?"

"Yeah," Al said. "It'd be great to catch up." The truth was, they hadn't exactly been friends, but then they hadn't been enemies, either. They'd just moved in the same circles.

"He's usually around the gym somewhere when he's here," Killian said, leading the way through to the back. "You're lucky you caught him. He's rarely here. Usually he's in Florida."

"Yeah," said Al, "I heard he's doin' miracles in real estate down there."

Killian nodded. "He's a very successful man."

Benny was uncharacteristically quiet, which suited Al very well. Usually Benny would have launched into long stories about the old days in the Mafia, and Al was exceptionally glad he'd neglected to do so this time. The last thing they needed was for their trip to be cut short.

They walked down a long, wide, brightly-lit corridor with a shining tiled floor that looked more suited to a hotel than a gym, and finally came to a large set of glass double doors. Through these, they saw a very large workout area, with treadmills, cross-trainers, a weights area, and all other kinds of fitness machines. There were numerous people working out. The business was obviously doing well.

Killian pushed the door open. "There he is," he said, nodding to the large figure in the weights area, lifting a barbell with huge weights stacked on either end. There was a beautiful female trainer, with a svelte figure and a long dark ponytail swishing down her back cheering him on. Porky pushed his arms into the air, locking his elbows, so the barbell was right above his head. He strained, his face, turning red, then purple, as the trainer counted down from ten to one.

"Zero!" she said, and Porky dropped the weight.

"Impressive, huh?" Killian said.

"Yeah, very," Al said.

The trainer then leaned forward and kissed Porky on the lips.

Al laughed. "Are all the trainers that friendly, or jes' with the boss?"

"I should be so lucky! No, that's Mr. Richard's girlfriend, Chelsea. Well, actually, fiancée, I guess I should say. He proposed last night."

Porky, feeling them looking at him, stared back at them. His eyes widened and he waved at Al, though he looked more surprised than happy to see him. "Killian, come over here," he said.

Killian jogged over, spoke with Porky for a moment, then jogged back. "He says to meet him at the juice bar in five minutes."

"Sure," Al said. "Where is it?"

"Back through the corridor, second door on the left. I'll take you there, if you'd prefer."

"Nah, that's fine," Al said. "We got it. Sounds easy enough."

"Great," said Killian. "Is there anything else I can do for you?"

Al shook his hand. "Nope. Ya' been real helpful."

Al and Benny went back through the glass doors and set off down the corridor.

"Juice bar," Benny scoffed. "A bar without alcohol isn't fit to carry the name, if you ask me."

Al elbowed Benny in the belly. "Well, it's clear ya' ain't used to any customs of the gym. This is probably the first time ya' ever set foot in one."

"You're not exactly Arnold Schwarzenegger yourself," Benny said, then sniffed.

"True," Al said. "But that's 'cuz of Cassie's cookin'. Benny, you shoulda' been at my funeral. The food was great. The pizza had one of them creamy white sauces on it. Man, oh, man it was good," He elbowed him again. "But ya' didn't come to my funeral. That's low, Benny. Real low."

"And I won't be going to the real one unless it's somewhere interesting," Benny said. "Go retire to your place in the Caymans, or some other exotic location, and I'll be the chief mourner. Otherwise I won't bother."

"Charmin'," Al said, then pointed to a sign on a door that read "Juice Bar" and grinned. "Look, yer' favorite place."

Benny rolled his eyes as they went in. "These millennials."

Al laughed out loud. "Porky ain't no millennial and neither is Killian."

"No, but you can bet this was a millennial's idea. We'll be drinking a kale and avocado smoothie in a moment, I can assure you. Well, maybe you will be, but I'm not touching any of that muck, Al."

"I know the word 'healthy' sounds like a disgustin' disease to ya', Benny. Don't worry, ain't forcin' ya' through the torture of fruit and vegetables, ya' know, healthy things."

Benny's eyes flicked toward his ankle, where he had his gun strapped on under his wide leg trousers. "Good," he said. "A smart man wouldn't dare."

Even though it was intended as a joke, it brought Al back to the seriousness of the moment. The juice bar didn't have individual tables, but instead had sleek long white tables that ran almost the entire length of the room, with chairs on either side.

Al slid into one and gestured for Benny to sit next to him. "Better if yer' at the side," he said. "That way Porky can be opposite, and we can talk properly." He lowered his voice. "Ya' think he had a good reason to kill Shirley?"

"Of course!" Benny said, far too loudly. "She tried to kill him!"

"Keep yer' voice down! Course I know that, but it was a pretty long time ago, wasn't it?"

"Yeah, but still."

"What about me? Why would he wanna' take me out?"

"People have their reasons, Al. Maybe you messed around with him back in the day."

"I never did nuthin' like that."

"But maybe he sees it that way. Or someone double-crossed him and blamed it on you. Maybe he got some false info. You know how it is. I don't have to school you."

"Yeah," Al said. Too many thoughts were bunching up in his head and confusing him. He stood up. "Whad'ya wanna' drink?"

"Strong coffee with four sugars, full fat cream, and a generous dash of whiskey," Benny said. "You know my style already."

Al chuckled. "Ain't gonna' happen here."

He scanned the board behind the counter, and there was no coffee on it. The only hot drink they had was green tea, and Al couldn't stand the stuff. He knew Benny would go nuts if Al brought him back a cup of it, so. he grabbed two bottles of sparkling water and got two glasses.

"You'll hafta' make do with this," he said, placing them down in front of Benny.

"Tasteless," Benny said, screwing up his nose. He was about to launch into a long rant, but he was cut short by Porky's entrance into the room.

"Al! Benny!" Porky said. He wiped his face with a black towel, then slipped into the chair opposite them. He shook hands with both of them. Though he smiled, the look in his eyes was guarded.

"Hi, Porky," Al said. "Good to see ya'."

Porky was direct. "What's this about? I hope it ain't no Mafia stuff. I'm out of the game. So far out of the game I'm not in the stands, not in the stadium, not even in a ten mile radius. When I say out, I mean out."

"Good to hear," Al said. "Me too. Or I'm tryin' to be."

"Heard you had a funeral," Porky said, then snorted. "Maybe I should do the same. But I have to come back and check on this gym from time to time. So, what is this all about?"

"Long story," Al said. "Short version is there's a hit out on me. Think it might be connected to Shirley's murder. Whad'ya think?"

"How should I know?"

"Well… ya' was so involved with Shirley, and ya' was kind of in on all that went on," Al said. "Thought ya' might have some info."

"I don't think so," Porky said.

"You'd have a great motive to kill Shirley," Benny said directly.

Porky drew up his lip in disgust. "Don't be ridiculous. I was at her funeral. You think that would have been a good move if I killed her?"

"Actually, yes," Benny said. "A great cover."

Porky was getting purple in the face, like he'd been when he was lifting weights.

"I ain't accusin' you," Al said.

"Only a bitter twisted man could have done such a thing," Porky said. "And that's not me. I'm engaged to a hot young gym trainer in the prime of her life. You think that's the kind of man who goes around murdering exes from years ago?"

"Congrats on that," Al said. "Heard ya' got engaged jes' last night."

Porky beamed. "Yes. Thank you. The women in Florida all turned out to be gold diggers, or the ones I met, anyways. Nothing against Florida. I make great money there. I certainly never expected to find a good girl here in Chicago. Real wife material. But Chelsea came in for an interview a couple of years ago, and I decided to take the interview because I wasn't happy with the hiring process. They kept hiring gorgeous stupid people. But Chelsea is exceptionally intelligent. That's the kind of woman I need."

"Know what ya' mean," Al said. "I'm married now to a lady called Cassie. She's wonderful. And she ain't affiliated."

"Good for us," Porky said. "No more dangerous Mafia women. Shirley was very close to killing me. I won't lie, it played on me for a long time. The love she showed seemed to be so genuine. But it was all fake, of course. I spent a lot of time wishing it had been real. I even struggled to be angry with her at times, as if she'd never tried to kill me at all. That's why I went to her funeral. I loved her, in spite of all of it."

"You're crazy," Benny said. "No wonder you were a target for her. You're too soft hearted."

"Did you just come here to insult me? As it happens, a lot of people loved Shirley. How do you even know she wanted to kill all those people? It was orders from higher-ups. She'd have probably been killed herself if she hadn't done it. Maybe that's what happened this time."

"Got any ideas who mighta' done it?"

"No," Porky said. "I was scanning the faces at the funeral, but didn't get the sense the murderer was there. Of course, a lot of familiar faces were missing, what with the undercover feds sniffing around."

Al chuckled. "They know Mafia funerals are prime pickin's for their Most Wanted lists. Probably were a coupla of 'em at mine too. Not that I was there to see 'em."

"Yeah," Porky said. Chelsea had just walked in and waved at them. He looked distracted, and clearly wanted to go over to her. "Is that all?"

Al was frustrated – no progress whatsoever. But he had nothing else to ask. "Yeah. Thanks fer your time, Porky. All the best with your weddin'."

CHAPTER SIXTEEN

"We're going to have to get some new flashy dresses," Cassie said as she looked herself up and down in the mirrored wall of the hotel elevator as she and DeeDee descended to the ground floor. "I'm sick of seeing myself in this."

"Really?" Dee said. "I'm still pretty enamored by mine." She made a little twirl in her dress, feeling quite silly and playful. "Though I'd never say no to more glamor. Normally I'd never wear anything like this."

"I used to dress up when I was younger," Cassie said. "It's been a long time since I've worn something so outlandish, although I can't deny noticing we've turned a lot of heads."

DeeDee ran her hand along her smooth updo. "I know. I could get used to this!"

"Jake and Al better watch out," Cassie said with a laugh. "We might just get snapped up!"

DeeDee gave her a playful slap on the shoulder. "Get out of here."

"Perhaps I'll find a handsome guy, say an investment banker, to whisk me away. One who's never been in the mob."

All of a sudden DeeDee was serious. "You're not serious, are you, Cassie?"

Just then the elevator doors opened and they walked out. Everyone stared as they paraded through the lobby.

Cassie sighed. "Of course not. I love Al more than anything. I'm just still dreaming of a life where guns and bulletproof vests aren't involved. Just my way of venting, I guess. But no, I would never leave Al. He's the first person who I can say has truly loved me on the deepest level. A level I didn't know was possible."

DeeDee felt tears spring to her eyes. "I feel the same about Jake." She quickly wiped her tears away. "Oh, look at me, being all silly." She thrust her head up high. "We're supposed to be power women, socialites attending an upper-class charity event."

"Thank goodness it's not affiliated with the mob, that's all I've got to say," Cassie said. "If I hear the word Mafia one more time, I think I might just lose it."

DeeDee laughed. "Oh dear. Seems like I'm going to have to hold you back from pounding someone's face in. I can just imagine you with your party dress, getting ready to savage someone."

Cassie smirked. "You're laughing about it, but I'm afraid it's probably closer to the truth than you may realize!"

"Ooh!" DeeDee said. "I didn't know you had such a fierce side, Cassie! Maybe you should have been the one in the Mafia. Oops. I said the word. Don't start pounding on me in front of all these people."

Cassie gave her a swipe with her purse, trying to look angry but laughing at the same time. "Don't you dare even start."

They walked out of the hotel and got into the cab that was waiting for them. Al had ordered it and treated them to a Rolls Royce ride.

"Woohoo," DeeDee said, when they got inside and shut the door. "We're riding in style."

Cassie rolled her eyes, but didn't really mean it. "Al's just doing this because I'm still just a little mad at him, and he wants to sweeten me up."

"Well, you sure got a catch when you snagged Al."

Cassie smiled. "I know."

It wasn't too long of a drive to the event, which was held at the Hilton Hotel in a large ballroom in the back. They sashayed through the front entrance along with the other attendees, feeling like a million bucks. Their Rolls Royce and fashion choices certainly drew a lot of stares.

"I hope we'll be able to find this Hope woman," Cassie whispered to DeeDee. "What did Benny say again? That she's an impossibly thin, tall, and beautiful brunette." They both looked around the crowd, tryin to spot a woman who fit that description.

"Well, that certainly narrows it down," DeeDee said. "Not."

"I'm also hoping no one asks us why we're here or who we know or whatever," Cassie said. "I feel like such a pretender."

"Oh, don't be silly, you fit right in!" Cassie gave her a look to show she didn't want to fit in. DeeDee chuckled at her. "Sorry, but you kind of do."

Cassie opened her mouth to reply, then stopped. She nodded toward the stage, where a very thin woman was sipping champagne and clutching a clipboard, while ranting at a large group of waiters. "Do you think that's her?"

"It's worth a try," DeeDee said. "Let's go and find out."

"Okay. We need to get our own champagne." She looked around, found a waiter, and took two glasses, then handed one to DeeDee.

They made their way towards the woman. "Now, remember," DeeDee said. "There's absolutely no way we can leave here with no information, like last time. I say we really push it, and if she's offended, so what? If she gets emotional, all the better. She might spill something by accident."

Cassie bit her lip. "I want to tell you you're being ridiculous, but you're not. That's a great plan." She let out a deep sigh. "Let's do this."

They both, as if by instinct, held their heads high and began to walk forward exuding poise and confidence. Cassie flicked her bouncing curls to the other side, and DeeDee smoothed her updo.

DeeDee decided to really go for it. She pushed through the huddle of waiters and waitresses. "Hi, Hope! So good to see you!"

"Oh!" Hope said, smiling. But soon her eyes dimmed of joy and became confused. "Hello. Yes, wonderful to see you." She broke eye contact and looked down at her clipboard. "You all understand, of course," she said to the wait staff. "Now, off you go."

Then she put the clipboard down on the stage and did a tinkly little laugh. "So sorry, you're probably wondering why I'm doing any logistics at all. Well, the truth is, I just don't trust anyone else to do it as well as I do. Terrible perfectionism, I know. But a girl's got to have standards!"

"Indeed!" Cassie said, smiling at her.

Confusion flickered across Hope's eyes for a moment. Then she said, "Wonderful to see the two of you again. We met at the…was it the Stafford?"

DeeDee grinned. Perfect. "I can't quite remember. I think so. We're staying at the Stafford now, aren't we, Cassie?"

"Yes, it's wonderful," said Cassie.

"You must have the afternoon tea," Hope said. "It's simply divine."

"We'll make sure to try it," DeeDee said. She edged closer. "Now, let me ask you something. Do you know anything about the death of Shirley Morris?"

Hope rocked back, clearly shocked by the sudden and unexpected turn the conversation had taken. Her brow furrowed. "Why do you ask?"

DeeDee looked at Cassie. She felt her heart beating with nervousness, but she'd already started, so she might as well finish. "Well, we heard she was killed or whatever. And we heard you move in similar circles." DeeDee took a deep breath. "And, well, we think she kind of deserved it."

Hope's eyes widened with shock, but then she slid into a glorious evil smile. "Oh my god, thank you," she said. "Shirley was so loose. She had so many husbands."

DeeDee nodded knowingly.

"Don't you think that's sad, though?" Cassie said. "They dropped like flies around her. She clearly hated to be alone."

"Oh, my goodness, you don't know?" Hope said. "She killed them all!"

Cassie grimaced. "Are you sure? I mean, we'd heard rumors, but..."

"I'm certain of it," Hope said. "That woman was evil. Trust me."

"Really?" DeeDee said in an excited voice. She was a great actress. "Did you have many dealings with her?"

"Not many, thankfully," Hope said, raising her upper lip in disgust. She sipped the champagne in her glass and left her red lipstick on the rim. "I tried to stay out of all that mob... Wait a minute... Are you... affiliated?"

DeeDee didn't know what to say.

Thankfully Cassie stepped up. "I'm married to Al, if you know of him. He was a big player around here before he got out of the game."

"Oh," Hope said, relaxing. She looked Cassie up and down, a little jealous, if anything. "Why did he get out of the game? Chicken?"

"No," Cassie said. "He just wanted a life where he wasn't worried about getting murdered in his bed every night."

Hope laughed. "He sounds like my Hank. Always bleating on about how we should retire somewhere. Ridiculous. I'm so sorry for you. It must be so sad to have a man without a backbone."

Cassie was getting red in the face. "I think you'll find..."

DeeDee laughed to smooth things over. "Seems you like life in the fast lane, Hope."

Hope fixed them both with an icy glare. "Why, don't you?" Then she turned to DeeDee. "What does your husband do?"

"He's a private investigator, but not anywhere around here. It's still pretty exciting, though, I have to admit."

As if for no reason, Hope burst into tears. "Sorry, sorry," she said, unable to stop herself.

"Oh, quick, come on," DeeDee said, taking Hope's arm. "Let's go to the ladies room. Let's go before people start noticing." She knew Hope would be embarrassed to be seen crying in public.

"Sorry," Hope said again, wiping her eyes. "I'm being so

ridiculous." But then she burst into a fresh round of sobs.

When they arrived in the ladies room, thankfully it was empty. Hope took one look at herself in the mirror and said, "Look at me. I'm a mess."

"What's wrong?" DeeDee asked kindly. "And by the way, you still look beautiful."

"Thank you," Hope said, sniffing. She grabbed a paper towel and dabbed under her eyes. "It's just... well, I've been married thirty years to Hank, and he's so totally and utterly boring." She burst into tears again.

DeeDee felt a little annoyed with her. It was clear she wanted some fast gangster life, and was mad at her husband for not providing it. It seemed very silly and childish. DeeDee could see Cassie out of the corner of her eye, pacing the floor of the ladies room, looking even more irritated.

"Oh dear," DeeDee said, not quite knowing what to say.

But that didn't matter, because Hope had plenty to pour out. "Sometimes I wish he was dead. The truth is I hated Shirley. She had all these different men and so much excitement. It's not fair! I mean, she was probably a six on the looks scale, maybe a seven on a good day. And I'm probably like a nine. Maybe even a ten when I'm not crying. And I got stuck with Hank, the most boring man in the universe. He's not even good looking." Tears streamed down her cheeks. "This can't be my life."

"Well, you can always change it, can't you?" DeeDee said. "You may not be twenty anymore, but you're gorgeous and well-connected and charming." She was embellishing a little with the charming part, but she imagined Hope could turn it on when she wanted to.

"But that's just it. I can't." Hope said. She looked around the ladies room to make sure no one else was there. "I've had numerous affairs over the years trying to make Hank jealous. Hoping he might fight for me, maybe even kill someone for me. But he never did. He just turned a blind eye. You see what I mean? He's like a dead fish at a fish market."

"If you don't mind me asking," DeeDee said, "why did you marry him in the first place? He doesn't really sound like your type."

"Well, let me start at the beginning," Hope said. "I'm not actually from a Mafia family. I was just a regular Chicago suburb girl. Well, my family had some wealth. But I wanted more. So I started mixing with Mafia types. I met this man called Vinny Santora…"

DeeDee and Cassie looked at each other.

"What?" Hope said.

"Well, he was one of Al's best friends," Cassie said.

"Oh, right," Hope said, quite uninterested. "Who's Al again? Anyway, it doesn't matter." Her eyes went quite dreamy. "Vinny Santora. He was gorgeous. So exciting. When he walked down the street, everyone turned to stare. I wanted to marry him.

"But he was too difficult to pin down. All the girls were after him, and as soon as I got one away from him, there was another one waiting in the wings. I finally told him, it's me alone, or all of them without me. And he chose them."

"I'm sorry," said DeeDee. "That must have hurt."

"But as a kind of a parting gift, he told me the higher-ups were advertising a job opening to run a hair salon and keep an eye on any Mafia news. I didn't know anything about hairdressing but I decided that since I was so glamorous, they'd pick me anyway, and I could just learn on the job."

"But they picked Shirley," DeeDee said.

A dark cloud passed over Hope's face. "Yes. They said I was too bland. Too bland? Me? Can you believe it? I was furious. I wanted to march back there and tell them all about me and how totally not bland I really was, but this guy called Hank, who they'd sent to give me the message, told me not to. And I sort of fell into his arms because he said some nice things. After that, I thought, well since he's Mafia, that's good enough.

"I rushed into it because I wanted to marry into the mob so desperately. It's the biggest regret of my life. I should have fought for Vinny. But I didn't, and I lost him, just like I lost the salon job. Although I don't know what I'd have done when they ordered me to kill my husbands. I'm pretty squeamish, to be honest. In Hank's early days, when he was a little more exciting, he had some altercations and I had to clean him up. To be honest, I vomit at the sight of blood."

She laughed bitterly. "Some Mafia wife I am. Maybe they were right. Maybe I am bland and perfectly suited to dull old Hank." She sighed deeply. "Wow, I'm not sure where all that came from." She gave a jittery, nervous laugh. "You won't tell anyone, will you?"

"Of course not!" DeeDee said.

Hope was beginning to look embarrassed, as if she regretted spilling so much of her emotions. "Okay, well, I think I'd better get back to the party. See you soon, I'm sure." She hurried out of the ladies room without even waiting for them.

Cassie and DeeDee stared at one another wide-eyed for a moment.

"I don't think she killed Shirley," DeeDee said.

"Why not?"

"Well, she said she was squeamish and vomited at the sight of blood. There was no way she could have jammed those scissors in Shirley's chest. That's not job for someone who's squeamish."

126

CHAPTER SEVENTEEN

That night, they stayed up late in their Langham suite, making plans. Along with DeeDee, Cassie, Jake and Al, Benny, Little Fingers, and Joey were in attendance, too. Al was annoyed they'd made so little progress and wanted to do something a little more special for the remaining suspects, Surly Sab and Rocco.

"I'm starving," Cassie said. "There were some canapes at the charity event, but nothing substantial."

They didn't feel like any of the dishes on the Langham's menu, so they ordered take-out Indian food instead. Al ordered the feast for ten, considering everyone said they were hungry.

"Okay, so Surly Sab," Al said, once the food had arrived. He tore his naan bread and dipped it in korma sauce. "He's too dangerous for me to go to his house, and anyways, he'd just throw me out or worse. We need a better plan."

"Yeah," Little Fingers said. "That guy would shoot first and ask questions later."

Cassie and DeeDee gave each other a meaningful look.

"What Ima thinkin' is to meet him at the private investment brokerage," Al said. "He's a partner. Ima thinkin' go wild with a major deposit. Like… $100 million. That way all the partners'll be there and he can't off me."

"Hate to break it to you, darling," Cassie said. "But we don't have $100 million."

"Aha, but that's where we come in," Little Fingers said with a grin, pointing at himself and Joey. "A Mafia man's always gotta' have some fake papers."

Cassie put her hand up, palm facing them. "I won't ask."

"You'll have to use a fake name," Benny said. "That Sab guy don't like you one little bit, I've heard."

"And a fake face and a fake body," Al said with a laugh.

"What about… if I go?" Jake suggested. "Make the appointment in my name, and I'll handle everything. Benny, you're coming, right? With the gun?"

"Nothin' doin'," Benny said. "That guy hates me too. You'll have to carry it. Anyway, I've got someone else to meet. I'm working on another angle to find out who killed Shirley."

He and Al looked at each other meaningfully.

Jake took a deep breath. "I'll take the gun, too. Anything to help. But why do you think this meeting is a good idea?"

"It'll be the only way to get him talkin' without shootin'," Al said. "With all the partners there, he ain't gonna' go straight in for the kill if ya' start askin' questions. Now, I dunno' if he's the one who wants to kill me, but the guy's very sensitive and very trigger happy. I mean that dude is one truly dangerous man. Don't make no comments 'bout his face."

Little Fingers shuddered. "You know that guy Valentino, he made a joke once at a social gatherin' 'bout his face. He was never seen again. Literally. He disappeared, and no one heard from him. Rumor was he was tossed in the river with weights on his ankles. But who knows?"

DeeDee frowned. "This guy sounds crazy. Jake, I know you're very experienced, but this one's making me feel nervous."

"Me too," Cassie said.

"It will be fine," Jake said decisively. "This is the next line of investigation. Let's just be brave and do it. Who knows, this might help us wrap up the case. We can't back down now."

Al clapped him on the back. "Good man. Jake, I'll ride along with ya' in the cab and then wait in it while you go into yer' meetin' with the fake cash."

"Right," Little Fingers said. "Joey and me are gonna' go organize the fake money tonight."

"Fred Marino doin' it?" Al asked. He remembered the name from the past.

"You got it," Joey said.

Al nodded. "Hope he's got enough for $100 million. That's enough fake paper to bring down a forest."

"We'll get as much as we can," Little Fingers said. "Bulk out the bottom of the suitcases with regular paper if we have to. Toilet paper, even." They both pulled on their coats, said their goodbyes, and left.

Benny shook his head. "This is kind of a crazy plan, Al. It's still not too late for you and your lady to hop on a plane to Venezuela, or Bali, or New Zealand, you know. Get lost in a crowd somewhere. I can do some fake passports for you, easy as anything. Start a whole new life."

Al looked inquiringly at Cassie.

"No," she said, holding her head high. She even managed to smile a little. "We don't want to live a life in hiding, do we, Al? We'd feel like we couldn't come back to the U.S., or maybe people would even track us down abroad. I think it's better if we just get this over and done with, right here and now, hand the culprit over to the police, and move on with our lives.

"Yes, this is scary and complicated, but we've come so far now, we might as well finish it. I want Al to be able to move on without this hanging over his head like a dark cloud." She looked directly at him. "You've had enough stress and danger in your life already, darling. I don't want you to have that for the rest of your life. Let's just get this done, and then we can live our happily ever after."

Al smiled. "That's my lady."

She sighed. "I'm really sorry about the things I said before. And especially about taking my wedding ring off." She twisted her finger and the ring flashed in the light. "I'll never take it off again. I was just, well, I was afraid. I didn't want this kind of life for us. But when I'm being fair, I know that you don't, either. In fact, this is the last thing you wanted to happen."

"Ya' got that right," Al said. "I'm livin' my worst nightmare. Always was in the back of my mind that some goon from the mob'd catch up with my new life and have some kinda' problem with it. And sure 'nough, that's exactly what's happened."

Cassie nodded. "But we'll get through it. We will." She flashed a smile. "And it'll make a brilliant story for dinner parties."

Everyone laughed.

"That it will," DeeDee said.

"Jake," Al said. "Ya' sure you wanna do this tomorrow? I'd never have asked ya', but since ya' suggested it, it does make sense."

"Of course I want to."

"Okay," Al said. "This Sab guy, his name's Sabazio Vinaccia."

"Let me guess," Jake said with a grin. "He was married to Shirley Morris."

Al chuckled. "Perhaps the only man in the world not to be married to Shirley."

"Why did he want to kill her?" DeeDee asked.

"Guy who threw acid in his face was Shirley's husband. But he was s'posed to be dead by then. Shirley'd gotten the order to kill him a long time before. Rumor was she didn't do it 'cuz he'd jes' lost all his money gamblin'. Dude would swing up and down, make a load of money, then lose it, then make it again. She was waitin' for him to swing back up, and durin' that time he went and threw acid in Sab's face over some argument or other."

"I see," DeeDee said.

"Guy's long dead now, but Sab had it in for Shirley. Always thought it was her fault, and it partly was. If she'd done her job, the guy'd never have been alive to throw the acid."

"Is he really badly disfigured?" Jake asked.

"Oh yeah. Had a lot of reconstructive surgeries, and it still ain't good," Al said. "Actually, it looks hideous. His wife even left him 'cuz of it. If I didn't hate the guy so much, I'd feel sorry for him. His whole life was ruined."

"Seems to be doing okay for himself, though," Jake said. "He's certainly got a top job."

Al nodded. "Yeah. Ain't sure if he's happy, though. Never remarried. Guy was a bitter, twisted man when I knew him, and word on the street is that he ain't changed."

"Swell, that's comforting," DeeDee said, looking at Jake with concern in his eyes. "Are you sure you want to do this?" Now she knew how Cassie felt.

"Yes," Jake said. "I'll be fine, honey. It won't be so bad." He grinned. "Plus, I get $100 million. I'll be a super rich guy for the day."

CHAPTER EIGHTEEN

The next morning, everyone was nervous.

Little Fingers and Joey came over first thing, with cases and cases of fake bank notes. "Fred Marino had everything we needed," Joey said. "Thank goodness for that."

Al arranged his tie in the mirror, secretly wishing that Benny was coming with them. As much as Benny liked to talk and complain, Al was always glad for his company, but Benny was working on another angle that he wanted to keep quiet about for now. It was possibly the most dangerous part of the plan, and Al was more than grateful to him for arranging the meeting.

He walked out into the main living area of the suite. There was a huge breakfast spread on the table that they'd ordered from room service, but Al was too nervous to eat. He drank his third cup of coffee, even though he was beginning to shake a little from too much caffeine when he poured it.

Jake walked out of his room in a designer suit and tie. He smiled nervously at Al. "Think I look credible? How did I make this $100 million?"

"He ain't gonna' ask questions," Al said. "He's the kinda' guy who knows money can come from all kinds of interestin' places. Any mob

133

guy does. I know the rest of them board members ain't mob, but if I know Sab, he'll be the one callin' the shots, no matter where he is in the official hierarchy. He's jes' that kinda' guy."

DeeDee, who was adjusting Jake's tie, said, "I can imagine how humiliating it must have been for his wife to leave him. He sounds like a very prideful, powerful man."

"Yeah," Al said. "With a very fragile ego and a quick trigger finger. Ain't a good combo." He tried to laugh. "Well, ya' know, that weren't a very nice inspirin' pep talk."

Cassie sat at the table, very slowly nibbling her way through a croissant. "You need to be ever so careful."

Jake patted the front of his waistband, where he'd put the gun. "At least I have this."

"Yes," DeeDee said, even though she was very worried.

The Gambinos left first, saying they'd be on call if anyone needed anything, and Al and Jake left shortly afterward in a cab, leaving Cassie and DeeDee in the hotel suite alone.

DeeDee, feeling insecure, double locked the door from the inside. She was still wearing slippers and a robe as she padded over to the table to try to eat something. "I feel so nervous," she said. "I don't really want to eat."

"Me neither," Cassie said. "But still I'm trying. I figure empty stomachs are only going to make us more anxious."

"You're probably right." DeeDee took a pineapple cream cheese muffin off the plate of breakfast rolls and took a bite. "Cassie, this is delicious. Glad I listened to you. You've got to try this. Matter of fact, I need to tell Susie about it so we can use it at Deelish. Kind of an Hawaiian feel to it."

"Back to the guys. I just hope they're both going to be all right. I mean, I know they're tough and more than experienced. But neither of them is used to this kind of thing, and Surly Sab sounds like a monster."

"He does, doesn't he?" Cassie said. "At first I was feeling sorry for him because of the acid attack and the surgeries and his wife leaving him. But honestly, it's kind of beginning to sound like he's a horrible guy. I'm not going to say he deserved what happened to him, though."

"I wonder if he was like that before the acid incident," DeeDee mused, "or if he got that way afterward."

"Good question," Cassie said. Then she sighed. "If I sit here and think about it I'm going to go crazy. Do you think we could distract ourselves somehow?"

"It's going to be difficult," DeeDee said, "but I think we should try. I say some Netflix is in order. And when I get nervous, I like to clean and tidy. I know it's already clean, but maybe I can find some clutter around here that I can get my hands on. That usually helps."

Cassie nodded. "I'm going to take a shower and spend ages doing my hair. Give myself a nice blowout. I'm terrible at it, so it'll be quite a challenge."

DeeDee chuckled. "That's a pretty good idea, I have to say."

*****

Al and Jake had a long cab ride ahead of them, since Surly Sab's firm was on the other side of the city, and the streets were jammed with traffic.

"Think we'll be ridin' fer at least an hour," Al said.

Jake was feeling nervous, so he decided to change the subject. "So where do you think you'll go on vacation next?" he asked. "The Caymans were great, weren't they? Gotta' love the whole island vibe, the weather, the fishing."

"Yeah," Al said. "Maybe we'll do Antigua next. I've been hearin' some great things about St. Lucia, too. I dunno', maybe the Seychelles, or the Maldives. Don't forget, we still gotta' do that divin' on Cayman for the underwater treasure."

"I'd kind of forgotten about it with everything else that's happened. Anyway, those are great choices," Jake said. "DeeDee and I were thinking of going on a cruise. A tropical one, preferably. Maybe around the Indian Ocean, hit East Africa, places like that. I'm afraid my geography's not up to scratch. I'll have to do some more research…"

"Another idea I had was goin' to the mountains," Al said. "Somewhere in Europe. Ain't never skied before. Neither has Cassie. She wants to learn. Think I'd rather stay in some luxury cabin in a hot tub, keepin' myself warm with liquor and plenty of food."

Jake laughed. "I've never really seen the appeal of skiing myself. I just don't like the cold. Whenever I think vacation, I think palm trees and beaches, or at the very least some heat!"

"Couldn't agree more," Al said. "But, ya' know what, ya' gotta make the wife happy."

They whiled away a lot of the cab ride talking about nothing much at all.

When they were about fifteen minutes away, Al got a phone call. "It's Benny," he said. "Yo Benny. What's up?"

"Don't go and see Surly Sab!" Benny said. "Turn that cab around and get the heck out of there!"

"What?" Al said. "Whad'ya mean?"

"He's found out somehow," Benny said. "I put someone onto watching the building, and they've seen all kinds of mob figures going in there that shouldn't be there at all. He's got wind that it's you, it seems, and has got half the Mafia inside there waiting to blow you away. I'd say he thinks you're coming there to kill him or something."

"But how did he know? Somebody snitch?" Al thought through the people who were involved. "Little Fingers or Joey let on somethin'? Or Fred Marino?"

"Who knows?" Benny said. "All I can say is if you value your life, don't go. Listen, I think you should just get out of town. Forget all of this. Like I said, go live in some remote South American village and change your names."

"Man," Al said in exasperation. His head was spinning. He leaned forward and told the cab driver to take them back to the hotel. "How's things going with you there?" Al asked Benny.

"I'm trying to meet with someone, but he hasn't turned up yet," Benny said. "Hopefully it'll go better than what's happening with you. Listen, just let me finish up and I'll come and meet you at the hotel. Lock yourself in your suite and don't go outside. This is really heating up now. I'll ask Joey and Little Fingers to come sit in with you guys, too."

"Okay. Good luck." Al hung up the phone and explained to Jake what was going on and what Benny had said.

Jake shook his head, his face drained of color. "I'm thinking maybe Benny's right. Just get out of here. This stuff is too crazy if you value your life."

"Seriously considerin' it," Al said. He called Cassie. "Hi, ya' both okay?"

"Yes, we're absolutely fine," Cassie said. "Why? What's up?"

"Tell ya' when we get back," Al said. "Be there in a half hour or so. Don't worry, everythin's okay. Love ya', Cassie."

"I love you too, Al. Hurry up and come back."

"Will do, there's jes' a lotta' traffic."

Al was overwhelmed with frustration. He pounded the side of his fist against the car door while he watched Chicago go by at a frustratingly slow pace. What had he been thinking? He berated himself for coming to Chicago in the first place. For now, he couldn't wait to get back to the hotel, hold Cassie in his arms, and let her know that she was safe. No more of this crazy Mafia stuff anymore, he'd promise.

But when they got to the hotel, something was wrong. Something was very wrong. The driver slowed down as he approached the entrance, and Al noticed a man standing in a black uniform, a little ways down from where the doorman was stationed. He recognized him, but couldn't remember from where.

Then the cab driver stopped at the front of the hotel, and Jake opened the door to get out. Just at that moment, a sickening feeling made Al's stomach lurch. He grabbed Jake by the back of his jacket and pulled him back into the cab. "Shut the door!" he hissed, then told the cab driver, "Get outta' here. Quick!"

"What?" the cab driver said, starting to sound annoyed.

"You're getting' paid pal." Al said. "Jes' go!"

Jake turned towards Al, wide-eyed. "What's going on now?"

"A coupla' guys were stationed out front," Al said. "I ID'ed the first one. They're contract killers from the mob. I recognize 'em. Sab musta' hired 'em and got 'em to cover the hotel."

"But what about DeeDee and Cassie?" Jake asked. "Will they be okay?"

Al was frantic. He just wanted to grab Jake's gun, jump out of the cab, blast the Mafia guys, and then scoop Cassie up into his arms. But he knew he couldn't. He wasn't about to spend the rest of his life in jail. Cassie would surely leave him. He had to be smarter about it.

He tried to call Benny again, but his call didn't go through. Next he tried Little Fingers. "Sab's got the hotel covered," he blurted out.

"What?" Little Fingers said. "Are you sure?"

"Yeah, I'm sure!" Al hollered. "Got hit men stationed outside, waitin' fer me. How are we gonna' get DeeDee and Cassie outta' there? No one can go outta' the front entrance or they'll be a target."

"I'll have to see if there's a way in through the back, through the kitchens," Little Fingers said.

"We could just call the cops," Jake said.

"Nah, they won't be any help to us," Al said. "As soon as they know it's mob business, they won't touch it with a ten foot pole. Fer all we know, Surly Sab's payin' 'em off." He went back to the phone call. "Find the way through the back as quick as ya' can. Where are ya'?"

"Me and Joey are already walking there. We were at a café a block away. We'll work something out. Don't worry."

"Ima worryin'," Al said. "Wish I could do somethin'." He called Cassie. "Listen, babe, ain't nothin' to worry about, but I need ya' to do somethin' for me. Make sure ya' don't let anyone into the suite 'cept Little Fingers and Joey, okay? Not room service, not anyone. Right? And I want ya' to keep Red right next to ya'."

"What's going on, Al?" Cassie asked.

"Ain't got time to explain," Al said. "But everythin's gonna' be jes' fine. See ya' soon, okay?"

"Okay," Cassie said, sounding very nervous.

Just then Al saw that he had a call coming in. It was Benny. "Benny, Sab's got the hotel covered and…"

"You need to come meet me," Benny said. "I've got some news for you."

"Huh?" Al wasn't expecting that. "Where?"

"The green warehouse in the industrial park coming off 20th Street. Are you alone?"

Al frowned. "But you know…"

"Are you alone?" Benny asked very pointedly.

"Yeah, yeah, I'm alone," Al said. "I'll be there in ten minutes." He gave the driver the directions. "Somethin' serious is goin' on," he said to Jake. "Benny asked if I was alone, but he knows yer' with me. Someone must be listenin' to the conversation."

"Like who?" Jake asked.

Al swallowed. "Got a pretty good idea. Jes' make sure ya' keep that gun close, Jake. This was a part of the plan I didn't tell ya' about and it ain't gonna be pretty…"

CHAPTER NINETEEN

Before long, Al and Jake arrived at the green warehouse Benny had described.

"Wait here fer us," Al said to the driver as he stepped out of the cab.

"Not a chance," the driver said. "I've been listening and it sounds like you're mixed up in some dangerous business. I'm not sticking around to get myself killed, thank you very much." He didn't even stay long enough for Al to reply.

Al looked around the area. It was an industrial area that had clearly seen much better days. Half the units were abandoned, and they were so spaced out Al knew if they screamed inside the warehouse, there was no one around that would hear them. A single old van trundled past them. The only other sound was made by trash blowing in the wind.

"Make sure to keep yer' finger on the trigger," Al warned Jake. "Sorry ya' got dragged into this."

"Don't be," Jake said. "Let's settle this once and for all."

They made their way into the compound of the green warehouse. It was fenced off, but the fence itself was rusting, as were the piles of industrial and car parts strewn around the front of the building.

"Looks like this place hasn't been used in ages," Jake said.

"Agreed," Al said. "Place is like a ghost town."

"Why would Benny want to meet us here?"

"Dunno. Your guess is as good as mine. Said he had a difficult job to do. Some kinda' meetin' to try and work out who wants to kill me. But why here? Weird choice."

"Extremely."

"Better keep our voices down. Don't wanna' tip anyone off that we're here."

They picked their way through the area in front of the building, stepping over rusted auto parts, and trying not to make them clatter with a metallic sound that would alert someone they were there.

Finally they reached a side door, which was open.

"Be careful, and go slow," Al whispered to Jake. "Mattera' fact, release the safety on yer' gun and be ready to shoot, jes' in case. Or ya' want me to do it?"

"I've got it," Jake whispered back.

"Tell ya' what…" Al went over and picked up a sharp piece of glass that was laying among the rubble. He wrapped a piece of cloth around the base, with the jagged tip sticking out, and held it like a weapon. "At least I'm armed with somethin'."

They crept into the warehouse, which had a strong smell of dust and decay. So strong that Jake nearly gagged.

Al whispered, "Ya' go that way, I'll go this way. Be careful."

Al made his way past rows and rows of boxes, which were thick with dust, and had cobwebs strung out between them. He thought he heard a creaking sound, but then second-guessed himself. He turned a corner to find himself facing a set of metal stairs.

Just then, there was a loud smashing sound from upstairs, as if someone had broken a window.

Al wanted to call out Benny's name and see if his friend was okay, but he knew he couldn't. Instead, he held his shank firmly in his hand, and made his way up the stairs as quietly as he could. It was quite a feat as his shoes hit the metal on each step, but he managed it in near-silence.

Then he had to creep forward. This was the scary part. The only way he could go was through a door, and he was sure the smashing sound had come from there. He decided he didn't have a choice, even though he was so scared that adrenaline zipped through his body and he felt his blood pounding in his temples.

He kicked the door open, then jumped back behind the wall so no one could see him. He hoped whoever was in there would creep around the corner to find out who was there, and he could ambush them.

But it didn't work out like that.

"Whaaaaaaaat?!" someone yelled.

Before Al knew what was going on, Rocco Rosetti was in front of him, pointing a gun at his face. Al was tall, but The Rock was even taller and towered over Al. His piercing blue eyes were animalistic in their rage.

"Aha!" Rocco said. "Just the person I wanted to see." He kicked Al's hand and the shank dropped to the floor with a crash. Then he pressed the gun into Al's chest and said, "Come and say hello to your little pal." Rocco grabbed Al by his shirt and pushed him through the door.

Al looked around the dingy room, and saw Benny tied to a chair with a dirty rag gagging his mouth.

"Sit down," Rocco barked, gesturing at an empty chair.

Al did. For some reason, he didn't even feel scared anymore. He was more confused. "I don't understand."

Rocco laughed. He sat down at a table next to where Al was sitting and lit a cigarette with his spare hand, all the while pointing the gun at Al. "Don't understand what?"

"Why do ya' wanna' kill me?" Al said. "And did ya' kill Shirley and them two other guys who'd left the mob? What's in it fer you?"

"Don't play like you don't know I killed some cop. Shirley heard about it, said she was gonna' use it against me. So I went to kill her, but she told me she'd told a few people – you, Butch Zamora, Huey Polanski. She said it was no use killing her, since all three of you knew about it, too. I decided to take out the lot of you." He laughed.

"Shirley was lyin'," Al said. "I never even associated with her. My guess is she chose three people who she knew had left the game and relocated. That way it'd take a long time for ya' to kill 'em and get back to her."

Rocco snorted. "She thought she was smart, huh? Well, she's dead and smart now."

"Look, I ain't got no interest in whether or not ya' killed a cop," Al said. "I'm outta the game. Totally out. I'm only here in Chicago tryin' to save my life."

Rocco waved the gun and grinned. "Great job you're doing. Oh, by the way, you had a wonderful funeral. Your wife Cassie makes excellent food."

A shiver went down Al's spine. "Ya' were at my funeral? And in my house?"

"You bet," Rocco said. "I was hoping to catch you that night. I knew it was a fake funeral. But there were feds around so I couldn't do nothin'. It's a shame I have to kill you here, really. I killed Butch and Huey at home, so I could take as many of their possessions as possible. Turn your pockets inside out."

Al was starting to freak out now. He'd heard all the stories about The Rock. "Ya' don't have to kill me," he said. "I ain't no danger to ya'."

"Oh, I know that," Rocco said. "It would just be a shame not to take advantage of the opportunity. It gives me a nice rush. I'll feel on top of the world for days." He edged up close to Al, pressing the cold barrel of the gun directly against Al's forehead. "Ready to die?" he snarled at Al with a wild crazy look in his eyes.

CHAPTER TWENTY

Jake had heard Rocco yell as he was slowly making his way toward the stairs. He'd started to edge up them when he heard voices, though he couldn't make out what they were saying.

He had a bad feeling in the pit of his gut, letting him know something was very, very wrong. He raised his gun and continued to creep up the staircase. When he got to the top, he stepped through a doorway and into a large room.

Time seemed to slow down in his mind. He saw a very tall man holding a gun to Al's forehead and Benny tied up in a chair. He knew he only had one chance to shoot the man and save them both. He didn't want to kill the tall man with the gun, but if he went for a shot to the leg or the arm, then the man would still be able to shoot, and Al would probably end up dead.

He knew he had to make a kill shot, but in the millisecond he had to think about it, he realized it had been a long time since he'd fired a gun, and that had been at a shooting range.

Time sped back up again, and Jake instinctively fired at Rocco's chest. But at that moment, Al lunged forward, and the bullet struck Al in his arm. Al cried out in pain, but at the same time knocked Rocco's gun out of his hand and it fell to the floor. Jake didn't waste a moment. He rushed forward, kicked Rocco's gun out the way, and pointed his gun at Rocco.

But Rocco wasn't that easy to take down. He lunged to grab Jake's gun. Luckily, Jake managed to jump out the way. Just then, Al launched himself on top of Rocco, and slammed him to the floor. Then Jake piled on, too. Rocco flailed and fought and bit and cursed, but between the two of them, they finally managed to subdue him.

Jake pressed his gun against Rocco's neck and said, "One move and you're a dead man."

Al's arm bled all over Rocco. "Are you okay, man?" Jake asked with alarm in his voice.

"Adrenaline's still pumpin'," Al said with a grimace. "I'll be all right. Gimme the gun. I'm heavier. I can hold this idiot down while you go untie Benny."

"I'll kill all of you," Rocco said, spitting onto the floor. "Just you wait."

"Yeah, yeah," Al said. "Yer' jes' lucky I ain't still in my mob days. You'd be six feet under within an hour or two."

Jake hurried over and untied Benny.

Benny jumped up out of the chair where he'd been tied and stretched. "Man, you guys took long enough to get here! This moron nearly toasted me."

"I'll call the police," Jake said.

"Snitch!" Rocco roared. "I'd rather you kill me than call the cops."

"Well, that's not your choice to make," Jake said. "I'll call an ambulance, too, for Al."

"If you're calling the cops, I'm outta' here," Benny said. "I don't want them starting to poke their nose into my business. Make up a story that doesn't involve me. Tell them you came up here, found Rocco pointing his gun at Al, and snapped off a quick shot that accidentally hit Al in his arm. Then Rocco's gun got knocked out of his hand by Al and the two of you jumped on Rocco to subdue him. Okay?"

"Yes." Jake felt nervous. He didn't go outside the law, and it felt a little strange to be friends with those who did. But he knew that all in all it was for a good cause – to finally get Al his freedom, so he decided he wouldn't tell the police that Benny had been present.

Jake called DeeDee. "We got him!" Jake said. "We did it. Did Little Fingers and Red keep you guys safe?"

"Yes," DeeDee said. "He and Joey are with us now, and they said everything's under control. I'll get a treat for Red and reward him for it. What do you mean you got him? Who's him? Surly Sab?"

"No," Jake said. "It was this guy called The Rock, after all."

"Why did he want to kill Al?"

"Because he thought Al had information about him killing a cop. He didn't, but that still didn't stop him from putting a gun to Al's head."

DeeDee gasped. "How horrible. Is anyone hurt?"

"Well, Al got shot in the arm, but he's okay."

"That Rock guy did it?"

"No, actually, I did," Jake said awkwardly. "I was aiming for Rocco, but then it all got hectic, and I missed, so I ended up shooting Al. Don't worry, and tell Cassie not to worry. He's strong and lucid and absolutely fine. Once he gets to the hospital, they'll fix him up quickly, and we'll be celebrating the beginning of Al's new life before we know it."

Al grinned. "Al's new life, take two."

"We'll meet you at the hospital," DeeDee said. She hung up, turned to Cassie and said, "Let's get going. We've got to get to the hospital. Al's been shot, but he's going to be okay."

It wasn't long before the police came to take Rocco away, and an ambulance arrived to help Al. He was going to have to go to the hospital to have the bullet removed from his arm. A policeman went with him to the hospital to get a statement from him about what had happened at the warehouse.

Jake had to give his statement at the scene, and he was extremely nervous. He'd never lied to the police before, and certainly didn't relish the prospect, but he didn't see what other choice he had. He pretended to look confident and answered all their questions without hesitation.

It was all a blur, but it was soon over and done with, and Jake soon found himself getting a police ride to the hospital. He asked at the front desk where Al was, and made his way to the pre-surgery ward. DeeDee and Cassie were sitting on chairs in the hallway outside Al's room.

He ran up to DeeDee and held her close.

"Oh Jake," she said, falling into his arms. "I'm so glad you're here. So glad you're okay." Words failed her as she half-cried, half-laughed. "Jake... Jake... I love you."

"I love you too," he said. "So much."

"We're just waiting to see Al. The police are still questioning him," DeeDee said.

"Okay," Jake said. "Cassie, have you seen him yet? Were you here when he came in?"

"No," Cassie said. "We hadn't gotten to the hospital by then.

There was a lot of traffic in the block around the Langham. Is he okay? Really?"

"Yes, I'm sure of it," Jake said. "I can't believe I shot him. It's so strange. That's the last thing I expected."

"Me too," Cassie said. "I'm just so, so glad this is over, and we can go back to our normal lives."

Little Fingers and Joey came up the stairs and into the hallway.

"Jake," Little Fingers said, grinning. "We were just out having a smoke. I heard you're quite the sharp shooter."

"Keep your voice down," Jake said.

A nurse popped her head around the door. "Okay," she said. "The police are finished with him and you can come in and see him now." Her eyes widened. "There's five of you. Normally three is the limit, but I'll make an exception."

They followed the nurse into Al's private room. She left and closed the door so they could have some privacy.

Cassie rushed over to Al's bed and embraced him. "Thank heavens you're okay!"

Al's arm was in a sling. "Yep. They gotta' do some minor surgery to get the bullet out, but it ain't no big deal. I'll be outta' here in a couple days." He winked at Jake, then pretended to be outraged. "That's the man who shot me." He looked at Little Fingers and Joey. "Get him."

Little Fingers and Joey pretended to shoot Jake, their thumbs and fingers cocked like pistols. They all laughed.

"Seriously, though," Al said to DeeDee. "Yer' man was a total hero. I'd be pushin' roses if he hadn't been as smart as he was. He crept up the stairs in that ol' warehouse at jes' the right moment and saved me. I tell ya' that Rocco guy is a total psycho. All ya' gotta' do is look in his eyes."

"I agree." Jake said. "I could see it too."

"He was talkin about how he enjoys killin' and it gives him a rush for days," Al said, shaking his head. "Complete and utter nutjob."

DeeDee shuddered involuntarily. "I'm just so glad the two of you are safe now."

"What happened with Surly Sab?" Cassie asked.

"He got paranoid and wanted to take me out, right?" Al said to Little Fingers and Joey. "Benny knows all the details. Lemme' call him." Al got his phone from the side table, made the call, and listened to Benny.

When he finished the call, he turned to the others and said, "Yep, he heard it was me comin' to meet him, thought it was a setup, and arranged for all his people to be there to blow me away. And he sent guys to the hotel. That guy's thorough, ya' gotta' give him that. So, Little Fingers, how did ya' get those guys staked out at the hotel and waitin' for me to leave?"

"It was all because of Joey," Little Fingers said. "Thankfully he had connections with one of the guys, and explained the situation. They backed off."

"Thanks," Al said. "Well, all's well that ends well, I s'pose."

DeeDee laughed. "I guess, although I'm still reeling from the last couple of days."

"Me too," Cassie said.

"You guys better go 'cuz they're gonna' take me to surgery real soon," Al said. "But go back to the Langham. Have a party fer me, and I'll see ya' before ya' can blink an eye."

EPILOGUE

A few days later, Al was out of the hospital and on the mend, though he had to wear a cast on his arm, which he absolutely hated.

Al, Cassie, DeeDee, and Jake decided to spend a day on Navy Pier. They were going to amble through the Flower Show, which had come to the Pier, followed by a cruise on Lake Michigan. Then they'd have dinner as the sun went down. Since they'd been living the luxury lifestyle at the Langham, they decided to go for something distinctly less highbrow. They opted for Giordanos, the home of deep-dish Chicago pizzas.

It felt wonderful to walk the Pier without having to worry about any shady Mafia or mob characters watching their every move. Finally, they were back in their regular clothes, and all was right with the world again. In fact, the whole saga almost felt like a dream they'd just woken up from.

"This is beautiful," Cassie said, arm in arm with Al, looking over the view. "Do you ever miss Chicago?" she asked him. "Do you still think of it as home?"

Al looked at her and smiled. "Home is wherever ya' are. I'm so glad this is all over. And I'm sorry for draggin' ya' through it all."

She smiled back at him. "Thank you for putting up with my

outburst, too."

"Was nothin'," Al said with a chuckle. "I do like me a feisty woman."

DeeDee smiled. "Aww, you guys are making me feel all warm and fuzzy." She had her arm linked with Jake, too, and he leaned down and kissed her. The moment couldn't have been more perfect.

RECIPES

SALMON PATTIES

Ingredients:
1 lb cooked salmon or 3 five oz. cans salmon
2 green onions, chopped
¼ cup parsley, basil, or dill, chopped
1 egg, lightly beaten
¾ cup breadcrumbs (I like to use Panko seasoned breadcrumbs.)
3 tbsp. mayonnaise
1 tbsp. freshly squeezed lemon juice
1 tsp. Worcestershire sauce
½ tsp. garlic salt
¼ tsp. freshly ground black pepper
1 tbsp. cooking oil
1 tbsp. butter

Directions:
Preheat oven to warm. Mix all the ingredients together by hand but the cooking oil and butter. Using an ice cream scoop, scoop out balls of the mixture and put them on a cookie sheet. Flatten with a spatula to make patties and firm the edges with your finger. You'll have about 8 to 10.

Using a 12" frying pan, heat the oil and butter together over medium heat. Place patties in the pan, careful not to crowd and cook

3 to 4 minutes on each side. When finished you can either serve them and reserve the uncooked ones for another time or put the cooked ones in the oven to keep warm and finish with the next batch. Enjoy!

NOTE: I like to serve these with tartar sauce.

PAN FRIED STEAK WITH RED WINE MUSHROOM SAUCE

Ingredients:
1 16 oz. boneless rib-eye steak (Any type of steak will work.)
2 tbsp. BBQ seasoning salt (I like Monterey Steak Seasoning.)
1 tbsp. cooking oil
¼ cup shallots, rough chopped (You can also use a white onion.)
1 cup red wine
1 bunch green onions, finely chopped (green part only)
¼ cup fresh rosemary, chopped w/stems removed
2 tbsp. butter
8 oz. Baby Bella brown mushrooms, stems removed, quartered
1 tbsp. herbs de Provence
1 tbsp. corn starch mixed w/two tbsp. water to make a slurry

Directions:
Trim excess fat off steak. Generously coat and pat both sides of steak with seasoning salt. Lightly oil 12" cast iron frying pan and preheat on high. When pan is hot and a thin film of oil is sizzling, add seasoned steak and cook for approximately 3 minutes on ea. side for medium.

Remove from pan, cover w/foil, and set aside while sauce is prepared. Reduce heat, add shallots and mushrooms and cook for 2-3 minutes. Add green onions and cook for 1 minute. Add wine, increase heat to high and reduce volume by half (takes about 3-4 mins). Add butter, rosemary and herbs de Provence and cook 2-3 minutes.

Mix corn starch and water in separate bowl until well combined.

Slowly pour and stir into pan as needed until proper thickness of sauce is obtained. Cut steak in half and plate. Spoon wine mushroom sauce over steak and serve. Enjoy!

CHOCOLATE FUDGE POUND CAKE

Ingredients:
¾ cup unsalted butter
3 cups sugar
5 large eggs (I use jumbo.)
1 cup whole milk
2 tsp. vanilla extract (Don't use imitation. It makes a difference.)
3 cups all-purpose flour
1 tsp. salt
1 tsp. baking soda
¾ cup unsweetened cocoa powder

OPTIONAL: ice cream, powdered sugar, chocolate sauce

Directions:
Preheat oven to 350 degrees. Coat a 10" bundt pan with nonstick cooking spray.

Using an electric mixer, beat the butter and sugar together in a large bowl until fluffy, about 2 minutes. Add eggs, one at a time, beating well after each addition. Add milk and vanilla and beat until blended. Add flour, salt, baking soda, and cocoa powder and beat on low until blended. Pour into prepared bundt pan and bake until a skewer inserted into the center comes out clean, about 1 hour.

Place pan on cooling rack and let cool for 25 minutes. Remove cake from pan and let cool completely on the rack.

You can serve with ice cream or top with powdered sugar and/or chocolate sauce. Enjoy!

PINEAPPLE CREAM CHEESE MUFFINS

Ingredients:
8 oz. pkg. cream cheese, room temperature
4 oz. can pineapple chunks in syrup, drained
1 cup plus 1 tbsp. sugar
10 tbsp. unsalted butter, softened and cut into chunks
2 large eggs (I use jumbo)
¼ cup whole milk
2 cups all-purpose flour
½ cup chopped macadamia nuts
¼ tsp. baking powder

Directions:
Preheat oven to 400 degrees. Line 12 muffin cups with paper liners or spray with nonstick cooking spray. In a medium size bowl, cream together cream cheese, pineapple, and 1 tbsp. sugar until well combined.

Using an electric mixer, cream the butter and remaining 1 cup sugar in a large bowl. Add the eggs and milk and beat until thoroughly combined. Add flour, nuts, and baking powder and continue to beat until blended. (It will be stiff.)

Spoon 1 heaping tablespoon of batter into each of the prepared muffin cups. Top with 1 tablespoon of cream cheese filling and then spoon 1 tablespoon of batter over the filling. Bake for 15 minutes. Reduce oven temperature to 350 degrees and bake for 10 more minutes or until a skewer inserted into the center comes out clean. Serve and enjoy!

AL'S FAVORITE PIZZA

Ingredients:
1 pizza crust (I like Boboli.)
4 tbsp. olive oil
2/3 cup mozzarella cheese, shredded

1/3 cup blue cheese salad dressing (I like Bob's Big Boy.)
½ lb. pork sausage
½ cup fresh mushrooms, sliced
½ cup chopped fresh onion
2 garlic cloves, peeled and diced
2 green onions, chopped
2 tbsp. basil leaves, chopped

OPTIONAL: Pizza stone and pizza peel

Instructions:
Preheat oven to 425 degrees. If you have a pizza stone, put it in the oven.

Heat 1 tbsp. olive oil in a frying pan over medium heat. Add onion and mushrooms. Cook until limp. Add garlic and cook for 1 minute. Remove from heat. Put onion mixture in small bowl.

Heat 1 tbsp. olive oil over medium heat. Fry the sausage until brown, breaking it up by stirring it from time to time so it becomes bite size. Remove from heat.

Place crust on pizza peel or cutting board. Spread 2 tbsp. olive oil on crust and then spread blue cheese dressing on top. Sprinkle with parmesan cheese. Evenly distribute onion mixture over the crust. Scatter sausage over crust.

Transfer pizza crust to stone or put into oven on oven rack. Cook for 12 – 15 minutes. Remove from oven and sprinkle basil and green onion over it. Let sit for 3 minutes. Slice and serve. Enjoy!

Paperbacks & Ebooks for FREE

Go to www.dianneharman.com/freepaperback.html and get your FREE copies of Dianne's books and favorite recipes immediately by signing up for her newsletter.

Once you've signed up for her newsletter you're eligible to win three paperbacks. One lucky winner is picked every week. Hurry before the offer ends!

ABOUT THE AUTHOR

Dianne lives in Huntington Beach, California, with her husband, Tom, a former California State Senator, and her boxer dog, Kelly. Her passions are cooking, reading, and dogs, so whenever she has a little free time, you can either find her in the kitchen, playing with Kelly in the back yard, or curled up with the latest book she's reading.

Her award winning books include:

Cedar Bay Cozy Mystery Series

Cedar Bay Cozy Mystery Series - Boxed Set

Liz Lucas Cozy Mystery Series

Liz Lucas Cozy Mystery Series - Boxed Set

High Desert Cozy Mystery Series

High Desert Cozy Mystery Series - Boxed Set

Northwest Cozy Mystery Series

Northwest Cozy Mystery Series - Boxed Set

Midwest Cozy Mystery Series

Midwest Cozy Mystery Series - Boxed Set

Jack Trout Cozy Mystery Series

Cottonwood Springs Cozy Mysteries

Coyote Series

Midlife Journey Series

Red Zero Series

Black Dot Series

Newsletter

If you would like to be notified of her latest releases please go to www.dianneharman.com and sign up for her newsletter.

Website: www.dianneharman.com,
Blog: www.dianneharman.com/blog
Email: dianne@dianneharman.com

PUBLISHING 3/24/19

MIDWEST COZY MYSTERIES

BOXED SET

http://getbook.at/MWSS

Welcome to Lindsay, Kansas! A small college town filled with colorful characters... AND MURDER.

Little did Sexy Cissy know that her writing would become secondary to solving crimes ranging from a dead judge to a murder in Sardinia, Italy.

If you like a mystery with intrigue in foreign places, dogs, recipes, and good food, don't miss this Midwest Cozy Mystery boxed set by a two-time USA Today Bestselling Author.

Open your smartphone, point and shoot at the QR code below. You will be taken to Amazon where you can pre-order 'Murder in Italy'.

(Download the QR code app onto your smartphone from the iTunes or Google Play store in order to read the QR code below.)

Made in the USA
Coppell, TX
18 July 2021